T0159184

The

BONE
HOTEL

Also by Mary-Keith Dickinson

A Divine Scavenger Hunt
Down to Dust

The BONE HOTEL

Mary-Keith Dickinson

ARCHWAY
PUBLISHING

Archway Publishing books may be ordered through booksellers or by contacting:

Archway Publishing
1663 Liberty Drive
Bloomington, IN 47403
www.archwaypublishing.com
1 (888) 242-5904

Because of the dynamic nature of the Internet, any web addresses or
links contained in this book may have changed since publication and
may no longer be valid. The views expressed in this work are solely those
of the author and do not necessarily reflect the views of the publisher,
and the publisher hereby disclaims any responsibility for them.

Any people depicted in stock imagery provided by Getty Images are
models, and such images are being used for illustrative purposes only.
Certain stock imagery © Getty Images.

ISBN: 978-1-4808-8835-7 (sc)
ISBN: 978-1-4808-8833-3 (hc)
ISBN: 978-1-4808-8834-0 (e)

Library of Congress Control Number: 2020907940

Print information available on the last page.

Archway Publishing rev. date: 5/27/2020

For my father, Keith Miller,
who taught me to swim in deep water.

PROLOGUE

July 18
Cypress Bend, Texas
Journal Entry

Twilight folds into darkness, leaving the moon blurry behind thick, humid air. I am stalking my personal phantoms into unfamiliar territory. Earlier while out for a drive, shouts of raucous laughter beckoned to me from a public picnic area by the Medina River. Several teenage boys pretended to ignore me—showing off, bragging, and chugging too many beers while swinging on a frayed rope over clear green water. I'm not sure why, but their bold antics made the bands around my chest relax.

In the days before alcohol trashed my will to live, wild antics and drunken night prowling were my favorite risk-taking behaviors. With survival instincts numbed, I didn't care about personal safety. Now, after a few months of slapping myself sober, I sit alone somewhere in central Texas, contemplating how shaky and bizarre my life has become.

What will I do this summer without Micah and Dula? The two mother-orphaned children that I nanny on an isolated ranch, have been beating on my chest with tiny fists of need, worming their way under my crocodile skin. Little parasites. Their sharp sparks of love make me feel vulnerable and alive.

My portable citronella candle flame flickers and attracts flying bugs as wax drips onto the limestone boulder under me. The tall shadows of Cypress trees are giants, and for good or ill, they loom, surrounding me. Should I be afraid to be out here by myself? The waist-deep grass rustles as if someone or something is crouching, waiting to pounce. Did one of the horny boys sneak back to harm me? Screw it. I've given up trying to predict the next life-shattering moment.

One thing I've learned is that the Devil wears many masks—my father's face as he crept into my childhood room at night as well as the blistering grins of judgmental do-gooders. I still hide from the multiple expressions of failure that superimpose themselves on my reflection in the mirror. Even though I sometimes experience a shaky sense of peace, many of the shadow-walkers from my past still wander unexamined hallways.

One of the ghosts that haunt me claims to be my personal Celestial Guide straight from the Seven Heavens—armed with maps showing the way out of Hades. I know how crazy it sounds, but sometimes the words from this metaphysical cheerleader bring comfort.

If I have invisible protection, then why can't I sit by myself without worrying about getting raped, or worse? I'm afraid of so many things—being a woman, being alone for the rest of my life. Maybe I'm just afraid to exist at all.

CHAPTER 1

"What'll you have, hon?" says the pink-uniformed, bottle-black-haired woman as she pours me a cup of coffee—Patricia, according to her nametag. Perfectly cast in the role of skinny, middle-aged waitress in a small-town diner, she has a sharp voice, stringy neck, and vein-popped hands.

While I look over the menu, her head and eyes bob and dart, checking coffee levels and the cash register by the front door, one ear aimed toward the kitchen, as if she is gauging the sizzle of sausages. Pencil poised, she raises her meticulously drawn-on eyebrows.

"So, Patty, what's good?" I say in a cheery voice.

The air in the room shifts as if the other patrons have held their breath in unison.

Ding! "Order up, Miz Patricia," a cracking adolescent voice shouts through the service window.

Patricia looks slowly at me, head to toe, as if measuring me for a coffin. "I don't remember seeing you in here before." She speaks like a police interrogator, leaning on the table, her pencil fisted like a weapon. It feels like I am supposed to have a permission slip from my mom. Fortunately, I have lots of experience with cops.

"Forgive my disrespect, Ms. Patricia. My name is Hope

Delaney. I work for Mick Flannigan out at the World's End Ranch."

She crosses her arms and nods, rolling her eyes as I continue.

"I just dropped off his children at the Saddleback Dude Ranch, and I'm famished." I pretend to be undecided about my order just to aggravate her a tiny bit more. "I don't listen to loud music and promise to follow the speed limit. Anything else you were wondering?" *Take that, bi-atch!*

A man sitting at the counter chuckles into his napkin.

"You want hash browns or grits with those pancakes?" Without waiting for my answer, she snatches my menu. "You're Jack Flannigan's new girl, aren't ya?" She says it as if there is a long list of Jack's ex-girls written on the wall of the ladies' room.

"Grits. Wait, how did you know I wanted pancakes?"

And how does this woman know about my boyfriend Jack? I've only been working at the ranch for a little over a month and even though I know that the Flannigans have ties to Cypress Bend, I can't imagine who would have told her about me.

Patricia presses her lips together in a tight line, and a deep dimple appears on one crêpey cheek. "You look like a flapjack girl to me." Her play on words do not sound like a complement.

Like a six-armed goddess of destruction, she shows me her back, juggling the coffee pot and menu but still managing to bump the chuckling gentleman with her hip before disappearing into the kitchen. This waitress deserves a round of applause.

The man at the counter looks like he walked out of a modern Western movie—tall, bearded, and sunburned, with a plaid buttoned-down shirt stretched over a big gut and tucked into jeans. He twirls around on the stool like a kid and touches the brim of his faded Trophy Hunters cap. His wide smile exposes perfect dentures and dimples that connect to deep laugh lines.

"Don't let Patty get your goat, young lady. She's protective of the Flannigans, Jack in particular. Can I join you?" He gestures to the seat opposite me and sits before I reply. He reaches his hand across the table. "I'm Jacob Lindheimer. You didn't have a chance, just now."

"What do you mean?"

"Of escaping Patty's shakedown. She knew all about you before you even thought about breakfast. By the way, you don't have to call her Ms. Patricia—she was just messing with you."

"So, Cypress Bend has a small-town psychic network?"

"Nothing psychic about gossip." Patty's my wife and she is the reigning Queen."

"Are condolences in order?"

Jacob's coughed-out laugh leads to the customers turning around again. "Pretty *and* cheeky. Poor Jack must have his hands full." His eyes sparkle, and I suspect he is old man flirting.

Patty returns with our respective breakfasts, plates balanced up to her elbow. Like a Vegas dealer, she distributes the food, utensils, syrup, and Tabasco.

"What are you barkin' at, old man? You're disruptin' my *real* customers."

"Amazing," I say, looking first at Patty and then at the delicious food.

"What?" she says. "You not used to seeing a hardworking woman?"

Jacob grabs his birdlike wife by the waist, pulling her close in a sideways hug. "Now, Patty-cakes, give the girl a break. She's complimenting you, not breaking the law."

"Just don't run my driver's license," I whisper as I take another sip of coffee.

"What'd you say, Hope? I think I'm losing my hearing." Jacob releases his wife. She pats down a few flyaway hairs before bustling off in a fake huff.

"How long have you two been married?" I ask to change the subject.

Jacob moves a huge mouthful of his chorizo-and-egg breakfast taco to one cheek and looks up toward one of the stuffed deer heads on the wall behind me. The deer aren't talking. Jacob is probably the reason they have ceased to roam the range. "Let's see ... I was born in '50, married in '67 ... oh hell, I don't know. A long, long time."

My pancakes have blueberries in them—an unasked-for addition but perfect with the warm maple syrup. Like little heavenly sponges, the pancakes soak up the sweet buttery mess.

Jacob nods toward my plate. "Good?"

I moan, rolling my eyes.

"If you work for Mick Flannigan and his lot, then you're bound to know Lanelle Lister."

"You mean Nell? Of course! She is like the Fairy Godmother of the Flannigan family."

Jacob glances toward the kitchen and lowers his voice. "Nell and I ... well, we go way back. We, uh, spent the summers together at her daddy's dude ranch—as counselors, that sort of thing."

"That sort of thing?" I say, slathering my grits with more butter.

"We were just kids. You know how it is."

"I think so." I smile.

Jacob's hidden walkie-talkie squawks from his belt, startling me into biting my tongue. "Portnoy to Chief, come in." No amount of static can mask the nasal-sounding voice.

Jacob shrugs, wipes the grease from his lips, and reaches for the walkie. "Go ahead," he says, standing up. I notice that under his nondescript hunting vest, he is carrying a gun, police issue, in a shoulder holster.

The whole restaurant listens as Portnoy drones on through

the static. "We need your presence down by the river, Chief. There's a problem."

"Again?"

"Sorry to say."

"Okay, on my way. Over." The big man sighs.

"Chief, as in police?" I ask casually.

Jacob nods. "Portnoy's a good deputy—takes his job very seriously, especially when it comes to keeping an eye on my wayward grandson."

Placing some money on the table, Police Chief Lindheimer gives me a wink.

"Welcome to Cypress Bend. Breakfast is on me."

CHAPTER 2

Almost like a case of Tinnitus, the vibration coming from my Celestial sidekick begins to hum from some other dimension inside my somewhat wounded psyche. I have finally overcome the knee-jerk terror that this voice might be an indicator that I'm losing my mind and have decided to view our supernatural exchange much like I would the inner voice of an imaginary friend.

Here we are in Act 3, scene 1. A mom-and-pop diner where a thirty-something woman sits alone in a booth after a palate-pleasing breakfast, stirring cream into her third cup of coffee in a thick stoneware mug. Our protagonist, Hope Delaney, having made an art of running away from pain, camouflaging her beauty, and avoiding intimacy, looks hip in khaki cargo shorts, leather flip-flops, and a loose black V-necked T-shirt; this morning, her long brown hair is imprisoned in a French braid. Not even the police chief suspects that she is really a jailbird and divine scavenger who communicates with the spirit world.

Cut it out, Oz-God, I say silently in my head. I can hear you even while pretending to ignore you.

How do you know it's me?

You whisper in italics.

I love it that you named me Oz-God.

Well, you are sort of a wizard—invisibly flitting here and there, chasing away demons, and trying to zap me with painful revelations of truth. Besides, The Wizard of Oz was my favorite movie as a kid.

Come on, you make me sound so dark. You've experienced a few good things since we met—a get-out-of-jail-free card, an interesting job, and what about Jack?

I'll admit your spontaneous entrance into my thoughts isn't as annoying as it used to be.

You did send me a psychic invitation this morning.

Not on purpose! And I know I didn't ask you to pretend we were filming a movie.

I'm your biggest fan.

More like my only fan. In the scientifically based world, you are most likely an illness or figment of my twisted belief system.

Dula and Micah are your fans too. How can you look into their trusting eyes and not see how they adore you? And what about Jack?

I've become more attached to those kids than I thought possible. And I actually get paid to homeschool them. Bonus! Now I'll be without them for a whole month.

Lots of excitement ahead.

I've stopped listening to your predictions. What's the benefit of having an omnipotent brain tumor if you only taunt and tease me? For once, can't you give me a clear picture of what the future holds? Something simple like 'Hope, this is the life/job/man that's right for you. Be fruitful and multiply.'

Free will …

I know, I know.

We've been dealing with the wreckage of your past.

Talk about a big-ass detour that I never wanted to take, ever.

I've mentioned Jack twice. Are you going to ignore me?

Maybe.

Are you sorry?

About what?

Me, in your head.

My suffering has been more interesting since you showed up.

Thanks for the endorsement, Eeyore.

Looks like rain.

You're forgetting the mushy stuff I offer.

Don't push it.

Patience, forgiveness and the times I cuddle your soul.

Stop. You and I talk. No cuddling allowed.

Ahh, such a rebel… until those pigs started to fly.

Don't start. Please?

Tsk, tsk. How did little Dula convince you to go tandem in her—what did you call it? That archaic ritual?

Her mother is dead, okay? They were all staring at me like I was a despicable heathen, and it seemed impolite to refuse. She had those baby tears on her apple cheeks. Let's just say I got baptized for her sake. What's the big deal?

You don't have to panic.

I looked it up. In Greek, baptism means 'bleaching a cloth clean and then changing its color.' Not religious at all. I can deal with that.

Very apropos. Kind of like Step Two.

Like AA?

Come on, you know how it goes.

Don't manipulate me.

Tell me, please?

Fine. The step says, 'Came to believe that a Power greater than ourselves can restore us to sanity.' You're certainly not helping in that department.

Righto.

That's all you have to say? Talking to a figment of my imagination doesn't seem sane at all.

Come on, give the Ghost a chance.

Doesn't mean I'm drinking your Kool-Aid. I will, however, acknowledge that recently, I've dropped pretty low on the divine food chain.

Humility suits you.

Shut up! You know I refuse to follow any party line.

Boxes, boxes, unwrap the boxes.

While we're on the subject, I'm still confused about what you want out of this … this thing we do.

Am I correct in saying that your fear of the spirit world comes from a limited and legalistic experience with religion?

Yes, but I'm over all that now.

Glad to hear it.

You don't believe me?

Hey, we're communicating. That's all that matters to me.

You think I'm prejudiced against religion?

Emotionally stuck is another interesting concept I heard recently.

Been spying on my counseling sessions too?

Unravel, resolve, and release.

What are you talking about?

Until you understand the situation you were born into, truth remains elusive."

So if I were born into a Muslim family?

Same process applies. Define your box. Remember, nothing about the who, what, and where of your birth is random.

Care to elaborate?

Denying your issues without knowing their purpose…

Makes me recreate the same shit over and over until I get it.

Such a quick study.

Then again I could refuse to analyze anything at all, right? You, or any being like you, aren't the boss of me unless I invite you.

Yep, that is how we set it up. I must follow the Prime Directive. You're quoting the fictitious code of conduct from *Star Trek?* Note how my eyes are rolling.

Truth is everywhere. We cannot bludgeon, stalk, or otherwise interfere with the free-will development of humans without an invitation. You want us to beg, right?

I'm not forcing you to do anything. You made up the bludgeon part.

Could have been wishful thinking. Organized religion almost killed my soul. I don't know if I'll ever get over that.

Don't worry, I speak many languages. Like what?

Math and singing and crystals. I love it when people plant food and flowers or paint, smile and hug or just sit quietly and stare at the wall. We can speak through everything, basically. You told me once to write this stuff down.

You express yourself creatively. So I'm just a tool you're using?

If I had a hammer … So what now?

I'd hammer in the morning. Are you going to sing the whole song?

I'd hammer in the evening, all over this land! Okay, I'm finished. No, you're not.

You're getting to know me. Survival of the fittest.

Saddle up, Kemosabi, time to make like a cow patty and hit the trail. Kemosabi? Native American references from *The Lone Ranger* are probably politically incorrect.

You continue to sass Oz-God of the Multiverse? Look around. I'm sitting alone in the flippin' Cactus Café stuffing my face and avoiding my boyfriend. Who else would I sass?

I like the stuffed deer heads.

All seven of them?

Dasher, Dancer, Bubba, and Bill …

Why am I in Cypress Bend?

Accusing the Multiverse of having ulterior motives?

Always.

Relax!

For the next month I have nothing to keep me sane.

I'm sure you'll think of something.

That's usually dangerous.

You have Nell's cabin by the river with your name on it.

Why can't I go back to the World's End?

Hello? Jack is in Cypress Bend. This is sort of a paid vacation.

Will you stop bringing him up? I was looking forward to some time away.

Are we talking about the same Jack Flannigan who jump-started your divorced heart and made you feel all toasty inside?

I'm getting swept away at an alarming rate.

Which scares you most, love, sex, or relationships in general?

I'm not talking about sex with a ghost—holy or not. In fact, thinking about you and sex at the same time makes me feel crawly.

What if I have access to insider info?

That's even worse. Besides, we all know what Spirit Beings think about sex.

Oh, really? You being such an authority and all.

What's your point?

Everyone on the planet has issues with intimacy—sexual and otherwise.

I'm not ready.

You and I have already discussed divorce, alcoholism, and sexual abuse. Why stop when we get to the good bits?

Forget it. I intend to eat this shit sandwich alone.

I thought you were a seeker, a divine scavenger.

Not today.

Grab my hand, little lady—we've got some fences to mend!

If you don't stop with the cowboy metaphors, I'm outta here.

Good times.

CHAPTER 3

"There!" Nell lets the sledgehammer thud on the ground and slaps her gloves together, reminding me of a middle-aged poodle kicking up dirt after marking her spot.

The three-story mansion looks slightly haunted, rising in charred elegance from the middle of overgrown acreage near the river. The building has a partially burned turret and dormers with other twists and turns in the architecture, indicating multiple additions over time. Warped and peeling shutters, once painted dark green, hang by a metal memory beside blown out windows.

"What happened to this place?" I ask.

"The police report indicated arson. They suspect a transient accidently set fire to something on the second floor."

Nell returns to the temporary sign she has just pounded into the ground. "Now, only one thing missing ..." Her clear eyes meet mine for a moment. Pulling a black magic marker out of her jeans pocket, she turns around and uses her petite body to hide what she is writing. I try to see, but she butts me out of the way. "Don't interrupt—I'm prophesying!"

"With a Sharpie?"

Standing up and blowing a wisp of gray-streaked blond

hair from her eyes, Nell steps out of the way. "Okay, smarty-pants, what do you think of this?."

"You're making me nervous."

"Relax, Hope, just read the sign."

I look and read aloud. "'CeCe Flannigan Adolescent Center.' CeCe as in Micah and Dula's deceased mother?"

"She was like a daughter to me and had a big heart for kids in pain."

"Well, starting a center in her name is a noble goal."

"And what did I add to the bottom of the sign?" Nell points.

"'Wanted: Director.' Oh no. Are you nuts? I have a job. I'll help you clean the place, but nothing else."

"You were a psychology professor in a well respected university!"

"Philosophy, not psychology, and 'were' is the key word. I got fired three months ago. That season of my life ended under a cot in a stinky jail cell." I shudder at the memory.

"That was before my dream," Nell says.

"Go ahead. Pull out your tarot cards. I'm getting used to supernatural crapola."

"Sarcasm can't protect you from the Almighty."

"Don't project your religious mumbo jumbo onto me."

"Hope, darling, I have dreams sometimes. They feel different from my other ones. I dreamed about CeCe's cancer before she was diagnosed."

"Do I even want to know what you're hinting about?"

"This sign"—she points—"I think the sign, this job, was meant for you."

"You're kidding."

"I may be pushy, but I've also learned to pay attention and be obedient to spiritual prompting."

"Like a well-trained pony," I say snarkily.

"You're just reacting to the word 'obedient.'"

"So?"

"Your sass can't dim your light, Hope. Cleaning up this building will be good for you, kind of like a living metaphor."

"Will I go to hell if I call you a bitch?"

Nell smiles and hugs me. "Sticks and stones ...."

"By the way, do you ever hear voices, in your head?" I ask, trying to be nonchalant.

Nell seems surprised by my random question. "What do you mean, like a schizophrenic?"

"Not like that ... here, let me get those," I say, hefting two jugs of Clorox into a wheelbarrow already loaded with a bundle of red shop rags and three boxes of industrial- sized trash can liners. "Where should I take these, Fairy Godmother?"

"Over there, my ash princess." Nell waves a jeweled hand toward the front porch and grabs a stack of empty five-gallon buckets.

"What do these voices say to you?" she asks, taking one sagging porch step at a time.

"One voice, actually. It's kind of like talking to a spooky version of someone I've known forever."

"Holy Spirit?" Nell asks.

"I don't know. Oz-God doesn't act too religious. Could I be possessed by something else ... something bad?"

"Love the name, 'Oz-God.' How do you feel when you guys ... talk?"

"Safe, whole ... connected. But I don't want to be tricked by some spirit-rookie miscalculation."

"God is good."

"What's that supposed to mean?"

"The creator of the universe doesn't need to trick you."

"But *you* can manipulate me all you want, right?"

"You're too savvy to be bamboozled, Hope, by the seen or unseen."

"Obviously, you don't know me very well."

Nell laughs. "The ranch has been a nice detour, but what about your dreams, your future?"

"I really love my job there. I'm not leadership material anymore."

"Destiny may take you in a new direction—just be open."

"Can we agree to disagree?" I ask.

"Exactly what are you being disagreeable about now?"

"Very funny. You are a traditional Christian who buys that whole religious package," I say.

"Lots of it, yes …"

"Well, I don't. Me holding Dula's hand while she got ceremoniously dunked in that preacher's backyard pool had nothing to do with me personally."

"Possibly, but you could look at it as a symbol of death and rebirth without strangling on a rosary." Nell wags her finger at me.

"Okay, maybe it was more than a dip, in a vaguely symbolic way."

"Sounds like you don't mind engaging in spiritual discussions, as long as you remain in control."

"So what if I want to stay on the ranch where I feel calm, safe, and sober?"

"Universal love doesn't work against you." Nell slips her arm around my waist and walks with me toward the house.

"How does *your* connection with the divine work?" I ask.

"I think that God is big enough for all of it."

"Do you really believe that? Usually, religious people act like cookie-cutter goose-steppers. I haven't been able to relate to any of you before."

"Your choices are between your own heart and that voice in your head. Just think about my proposal. As your friend, I want to encourage the strengths I see inside you."

"You won't hate me if I don't accept your offer?"

"Only if you break your promise to help me clean the place!"

"No, sir!" I salute.

Nell points to a large broken sign leaning against the front porch. "See that?" Moving closer, she points to the part showing the last half of the hotel's name painted in Gothic lettering. "The 'bone Hotel'? How fitting for a haunted mansion," I laugh.

"Pettibone Hotel." Nell whispers the name as if savoring a memory or saying a prayer.

"Pretty important, those Pettibones," I say. "What's their story?"

"My grandfather came to America from Germany in the eighteen-hundreds with a group of Freethinkers."

"Freethinkers?"

"My ancestors would be disgusted over the condition of this town." Nell stops and gazes at nothing, as if adding more renovations and projects to her mental to-do list.

"What did the Freethinkers believe?"

"Just the facts, or what could be scientifically proven—absolutely no support for supernatural phenomena."

"Supernatural, like God?"

"Yes. They moved out here in the country hoping to escape any interference from church or government."

"Ha! You come from a long line of unbelievers."

"Au contraire, mon cheri." Nell walks up the front porch steps and strikes a pose in front of the graffiti-covered door. "My grandmother was defiant—very much like you. One night she had a 'visitation' by an angel and marched herself down to the only church in town—Methodist, I believe—and told the minister all about it. Caused quite a ruckus."

Nell and I peek through a broken window. Old furniture, crates of magazines, a burned mattress, and some dismantled ceiling fans are piled almost knee-deep in some areas.

"So who was this Mr. Pettibone?" I ask, pushing the front door open.

"Titus Pettibone was the richest man in the county. Of course, Granny caught his eye, married him, and used his money to bankroll many of the original buildings here, including the theater Jack is renovating."

"So you're carrying on her tradition?"

Nell nods and then sneezes. She kicks the mattress in the entry hall, and a large rat squeaks and scampers to a pile of trash in the corner.

"With a little Clorox, a few throw pillows ..." She laughs at the scowl on my face. "One trash bag at a time, Hope."

"When was the last time anyone stayed here, the Great Depression?"

"Oh no, it seems like yesterday that this place was my castle. We lived here every summer during the 50s and 60s. I have so many memories, had so many friends."

"Like Jacob Lindheimer?"

She blushes. "How do you know about ... never mind. We have work to do."

With her face still red, Nell struts confidently through the mess, lifting unidentifiable rubbish here and there with the pointy toe of her cowboy boot.

"I know your secret," I sing, sashaying past her.

"I won't respond to your childish antics. Have some respect for your elders!"

"I could prolong this torture, Nell, or you could just tell me ..."

"Go grab those buckets!"

"Okay, okay!" I back off and we high-step our way through the remaining rooms on the bottom floor. "This is overwhelming! You know I only have a month to help you."

"I'll hire someone else—maybe Jack on the weekends. That should be fun for the two of you."

Expertly, I dodge the subject. "Do you really think I am qualified to help adolescents? Who would teach Micah and Dula if I left?"

"None of these issues need an answer today. Why are you avoiding Jack?"

"Good God, everyone is up my butt about Jack!"

"Ooh, touched a nerve, eh?"

"Our relationship is barreling forward too fast."

"He told me you were taking things slowly." Nell sounds concerned.

"He talks to you about me? Great."

I always forget how short Nell is because her energy extends about ten feet out from her body. She takes my hands firmly in hers. "It's time to come out of hiding, Hope, from life, from men, and most of all, from yourself."

"Thanks, Obi-wan."

"This might help." Nell waves a credit card in my face. "Can you say 'Platinum'? I've already arranged for a direct deposit into your bank account as well."

"How do you have access to my … wait, of course, I'm sure every bank owner in Texas used to date you."

"Bite your tongue."

Snatching the card, I return her fierce hug.

Nell walks down the sidewalk to her Mercedes SUV.

"Are you just leaving me here?"

"Don't worry, I emailed you directions to the cabin and the Rialto where Jack is waiting. Go see him!" She makes the sign of a phone with her thumb and pinky and drives off.

I look up at the building. The jagged glass and sooty window frames on the upper floor make the house look like a skull. "Welcome to Hotel Hell," I mutter.

CHAPTER 4

The property around the hotel is overgrown with wildflowers mixed with native grass and littered with trash, torn cardboard boxes, and mangled metal items. A few pieces of burned and broken furniture are grouped together in a haphazard circle—a hobo hangout under some huge oak trees.

I pull four trash bags from the roll and take the tags off the soft leather gloves Nell bought me.

Oh goodie, garbage!

Why, Oz-God, why?

Why what? I see at least six questions flapping like SOS flags in your mind.

Why this filthy, rat-infested pit of manual labor?

Hard work is good for the soul.

You sound like her.

Nell? We like the same music.

Why does she keep pestering me? Every interaction with her feels rigged.

Annoyed?

I don't want to talk about it.

Do you want me to guess what's wrong?

You already know!

Use words.

The things she says ...
Insults? Commands? Criticism?
Religion. She talks about prophecy and God's love. Probably wants me to *pray*. Christian-ese is worse than chewing on foil.
Keep talking. You can gather trash at the same time.
This is so demeaning ... I have more noble things to do.
Let it all out, I can take it.
Am I not allowed to have *any* pride?
This kind of work stimulates your naturally rebellious spirit.
You say that like it's a good thing.
If your issues hadn't slapped you in the face, would you have dealt with them?
No need for violence.
Did you listen to any still, small voice before your life ended up in the crapper?
I might have, eventually ...
Keep dreaming, dear one. I had to almost shatter your eardrums on the beach to get your attention.
That was you?
Body, mind, and spirit are connected.
If you say so ... I don't think Nell plans to lift a finger to help me with this job.
The nerve! What kind of monster is she, anyway?
I know ... bribing me with money, trying to force me into meaningful work, *and* interfering in my personal life. Jeez!
Are you going to pout all day?
I find it difficult to do work with no intellectual payoff. Actually, this whole thing is *your* fault!
How could I have been so insensitive?
Uhh ...
Snap out of it!
It's just that at the ranch, no one expects too much out

of me. This summer detour seems like a further demotion, if that's even possible.

Aren't you pitiful.

I'm suffering here!

You're exactly where you're supposed to be.

Don't tell me ... there are treasures buried in the rat kingdom.

Let's make a deal.

Cosmic deals are weighted in your favor.

If you mean infused with the infinite power of love? Most certainly.

What's the deal?

Try to set your pride aside for one month.

You want me to be grateful for this mindless slavery?

Mindlessness is a choice.

I guess that cleaning could be less excruciating than some of the other torture you've put me through.

Poor, pathetic Hope.

I suppose I could practice being grateful.

There are peach trees over there with perfect orbs of sweetness ready to be picked.

What do peaches have to do with anything?

Anything is everything ...

Whatever.

Certain thought forms open the heart center between your dimension and mine—connection doesn't have to be a certain ritual or a set of specific phrases said in rigid order. The intention or desire to seek unlocks the door.

Reciting ancient poetry is not my thing.

Time to take a peach break.

Are you manipulating me again?

Just go with it, for once.

I thought you wanted me to work, not eat peaches.

Living in the moment is difficult.

On the Eightfold Path?

On any path.

So universal truth *does* cross belief systems?

Thus the term 'universal.'

Aha! Then all religions lead to the same place!

'Universal truth' equals Source, i.e. the creator of every particle in the universe, which does include all religions, and every person. Different expressions of truth bring about different stages of evolution.

Sounds like you're avoiding my question.

What did you learn when you studied Buddhism?

To show compassion for all living things.

Including yourself?

Please shut up.

Would it surprise you to know that picking up trash or eating a peach can become a prayer?

But prayers are supposed to be words and creeds that petition God to do things in my favor.

There are many prayer languages. As with everything related to spirit, there is more to the story.

Our conversation is words. Am I praying right now?

What do you think?

But I'm not asking you for anything.

You can. We are supposed to work together.

Give me my daily pancakes?

What have I dished out today?

A big fat pile of ...

Contemplate your present situation.

You're making me tired. Right now I feel fear. No more children to buffer my feelings and distract me from going down the rabbit hole with Jack.

So to speak.

You are so bad! And now I get four weeks of manual labor, plus confusion about my future.

Today you have a place to live, enough money to pay your bills, a new and exciting relationship to explore ... and isn't that peach delicious?

Sublime, but—

What do you see, with your physical eyes?

Oh wow, you're really going to make me do this?

Imagine me raising my eyebrow.

Okay, I see other peaches on the tree—gold and red-tinged—with fluttering green leaves around them.

What about your other senses?

The peaches smell great, and maybe when I rub one against my lips, I think of my Nana's cheek.

What's that I heard?

The sound of one hand clapping?

Don't leave me hanging.

By the way, just for the record, I'm an adult. There's nothing wrong with me having sex with my boyfriend.

I love talking about sex ...

Wait. That's not the response I expected. You sound so creepy. Never mind. Forget I said anything.

No way.

Shit! I said I didn't want to go there with you! I'm leaving this plastic bag of crap, these fancy gloves, and this conversation right now. There better be a Dairy Queen in this freaking town.

CHAPTER 5

Junk food is my newest art form. Back when I considered myself to be one of the alcoholic elite, I drank far and wide, looking for the perfect libations for all occasions. For breakfast, I might order a spicy Bloody Mary, a Pimms and soda for an "aperitivo", then a burlap-covered bottle of Basque wine, Rioja, for lunch. Of course I chose aged Scotch or Tanqueray and tonic for everything else. What an idiot. By the time I crashed to the bottom of my life, even a few gulps of Listerine or Nyquil weren't off limits.

Today, I investigate fast-food venues like a connoisseur, savoring the different aromas of meat grease. The sizzle of various potato products has become a symphony with the final crescendo being sugar-laden ice cream treats.

Running away from my feelings hasn't stopped with sobriety; I just jump onto different trains still trying to escape them. Damn, this chocolate malt is good!

Your mind is a masterpiece.

Oh, you're back.

I want to remind you of something. I don't barge into your thoughts. There are times when your mental frequency changes and, whether you are conscious of it or not, there is an invitation.

Sorry about that brain-fart back at the hotel.

So, you want to have sex with Jack?

Not necessarily.

Now who's avoiding the truth?

Oh stop, of course I'm thinking about it!

What's different this time?

I've been a loose woman making bad choices for most of my adult life. That isn't working for me anymore. I don't want to ruin everything this time, yet I can't go backwards either. I feel trapped and clueless.

Thank you for being honest.

Discussing sexual behavior isn't too popular in your world, right?

How do you know?

I study these issues in my spare time … on the pot.

Learn anything?

Well, I started with the basics, you know, structured systems of belief.

You really hate the word, religion, don't you?

Most of the people in my world do.

What's your 'potty philosophy?'

Ha, good one. Several sets of spiritual guidelines overlap in terms of social interaction and basic personal growth.

Any rules about sex?

Not so much—just get married young and stay away from your neighbor's wife and handmaids. Oh, and don't spill your seed on the ground. Eww.

A, B, C, easy as 1, 2, 3.

Sure … but I was brainwashed.

Care to elaborate?

Black and white, right or wrong. If I failed at being good, I was bad—lost and going to hell. Then my father molested me, and any chance I had at redemption was ruined.

Doomed to fail?

I don't get it.

Get what?

It feels like both ends of the black-and-white spectrum are missing something.

Actually, they are inseparable.

Whoa now …

Why does any individual need laws or guidelines?

Duh, to have a functional society, besides, I like lists. The Twelve Steps and a class syllabus show me what to do first and what's expected at the end.

Could it be that you like the edges of 'right and wrong' for a different reason?

Knowing the rules makes me feel as if I have *some* control. I've rebelled against everyone in authority—enjoyed seeing how close I could get to the dark edge of disaster without losing my job or going to prison.

And then you stumbled over that center stripe.

Don't rub it in. I officially suck at escaping the consequences of my actions.

Be grateful. It's a gift.

This crap is too deep.

Chicken!

Bully!

Feel better?

Are you going to smite me?

Will you shut your gob and let me finish my eloquent lecture?

I guess that 'smite' and 'listen' are two sides of the same coin.

Dualism in action.

So you could smite me even if I listen?

Listening to me might feel like a smite. Boom!

You win.

Wherever legalism is worshipped, the interpretation of right and wrong remains in the hands of those in positions of power and control. Not necessarily 'enlightenment' or 'good news' at all.

At least no one can accuse me of being legalistic.

Are you sure? Don't you believe that if you had been 'blessed,' or been one of the lucky girls and not ruined from the start, you could have earned salvation, a lifetime sobriety chip, and a free ticket to happiness?

This conversation isn't going the way I'd planned.

Religious commandments are like rules to train children. This little piggy went to market, this little piggy stole a car, and this little piggy screwed his neighbor, then beat up grandma. Don't be a bad piggy.

Um, those rules are supposed to be written in stone, right? Sounds like you are disrespecting your own manifesto.

Discipline that comes out of love activates certain areas of the brain.

Okay, but—

I'll give you an example. When a child's ego locks horns with a parent presenting healthy guidelines, the process of soul-evolution can begin. Later the process of discernment is internalized and you decide what is truth for you.

How do I know that what you're saying is correct?

You don't. Does it resonate in your heart?

What a weird thing to say. No wonder people want a preacher to tell them what to do. Listening to your heart takes too much effort. What if my interpretation of God is coming from a brain tumor?

A fascinating concept to ponder. All actions and beliefs, along with their consequences, provide an opportunity for learning.

I'm so confused.

Knowing your ABC's is how you learn to read, but those initial steps only get you to a certain point. The letters of the alphabet join together and lead to something more.

Words become sentences, then paragraphs, books et cetera ... I get the metaphor.

What do you tell a toddler who is headed to the wall socket with a fork?

"Thou shalt not put fork in wall socket."

Which leads to ...?

Thou shalt not have premarital sex?

If I laugh any harder, acorns will fall from these trees"

Not *that* funny.

If you are breathing, you will make mistakes.

If I'm doomed to fail, why bother?"

"This isn't about being perfect or running amok."

Then what's the point?

Each rule or law has a key hidden in it that opens a door to a deeper understanding of things.

Can I lose my connection to you by doing something horrible?

Start where you are. Examine the acorns in your own pocket; then follow the map you were born with until you lose control. That's when you heard my voice, remember?"

Will I get better?

You have much to learn, young Jedi ... but our ways are written on your heart, not just hidden away on sacred scrolls.

Make sure all the people in my life get that memo.

Everyone has a different journey. Focus on your own growth.

I resent men and women who abstain until their wedding night. In case you forgot, my virgin ship has left the building.

Your mixed metaphor is delightful. Sex is a complex issue. What's inside that tradition?

I don't have the key!

Yoo-hoo! Hello? Is this thing on?

CHAPTER 6

Nell and her family own many riverfront cabins in Cypress Bend, but the one she chose for me is the cutest—small and well decorated with pecan wood cabinets, a full kitchen, and a wrought-iron bed by the picture window overlooking the waterfront. Cottonwood trees surround the cottage, creating a shady canopy. I suppose I can suffer here for a month.

Late-afternoon heat pulses against my skin. Maybe walking to the Rialto Theater wasn't such a brilliant idea. Even though I showered after working at the hotel, my face is already glazed.

Most of the buildings in the downtown area have an old-world German look, square and solid, often with the year of their construction carved into the pediment. Limestone storefronts, a corner bank, and an assortment of smaller shops line the street for more than three blocks.

I pick up an informative pamphlet about the history of Cypress Bend on my way past the library. According to some of the historical landmarks listed there, the Pettibone and Flannigan families have maintained a substantial niche here for generations. Nell's family built not only the Pettibone Hotel but also the Rialto Theater and the original high school. No wonder Jack accepted the renovation job—Nell probably didn't give him much of a choice.

My stroll takes me back past the Cactus Café. Glancing in the window, I see a woman close to my age sliding what looks like a large Coke and an order of home-cut fries across the counter to a young man slouching on the same round counter stool that Chief Lindheimer occupied earlier.

The woman wears a pink polyester uniform identical to Ms. Patty's. With the same height and slight build, she might be related. I stare as she playfully touches the boy's hand, wags her finger close to his face, and tugs on his shirtsleeve. A napkin appears out of thin air, ready to wipe his face as if he were still an infant. He swats her hand away and dips his head to avoid more contact.

My chaotic brain activity screeches to a halt. What would it be like to have a son? Was the baby I aborted a boy? The question hits me in the gut like a cinder block. When I was married to Steve, I never thought seriously about having a baby.

Do you feel the same way today?

You're peeking again.

So are you.

I can see how much that woman loves her son.

Even though he sulks and pushes her away.

I don't understand.

She loves her child no matter what he does. We love you the same way.

Must be nice to be on the right track.

Her story might surprise you.

Couldn't be worse than mine.

You don't have a copyright on misery.

Raising children is such a responsibility. I don't know why so many young girls want to rush into motherhood, husband or not. I can't believe I was so irresponsible about birth control.

A wisdom key has been misplaced.

No way would I bring an unwanted child into the world.

Then again, terminating my pregnancy probably wasn't the best plan either.

Babies are a consequence of making love. Life can be messy.

The waitress looks up and sees me through the window. She squints her eyes and stops smiling—her lips forming a line that reminds me of Patty, who, as if summoned, walks out from the kitchen. They glance at me and then at each other, and Patty nods her head. The young woman walks around the counter to the ladies' room.

What have I done now? I hurry past the café, acutely aware of my stranger status in this town. I don't need to worry about making friends this summer—the female ranks have already circled the wagons.

Oh no, I made a cowboy metaphor.

CHAPTER 7

Walking into the lobby of the Rialto Theater, I'm assaulted by memories of the past, not of a specific person, place, or movie, but of entering a safe, familiar locale that always provided sanctuary. Even today, I crave the air-conditioned blackness of a weekday matinee—my first and most enduring escape. No matter where a movie transports me, it's always away from reality.

Sitting in the back row of the auditorium, I watch Jack and his crew try to unhook a torn red velvet curtain from its track above the movie screen without pulling the ceiling down on their heads.

Am I watching the new movie of my life? Jack is the perfect leading man, a dashing dark-haired character with a quick temper and tender heart, trying to live up to the Flannigan name and overcome the shame of his father's suicide. His mother was born into a wealthy family in Mexico and, for Jack, the challenges of coming from a mixed heritage sometimes torments him. Will ours be a romance or a nightmare, a happy ending or a tragedy? God only knows.

I slide further down in my seat, trying to become more invisible. So far, Jack's confidence seems impressive one moment and shattered the next—nerve-wracking for someone as insecure as I am. Sometimes I watch in fear as thought-shadows move across his face like moody portents of the storms to come.

People like me aren't destined for healthy relationships. My personality is made up of the broken pieces of a life that nobody treasured. How can Oz-God encourage me to find purpose *and* date someone? The two activities seem as far apart as Cypress Bend and Tibet.

As if picking up my thoughts, Jack's gaze sweeps the room until he spies me slouched in my hideaway. With the grace of a track star, he vaults over a sawhorse and strolls toward me, letting his hand thump on each row of dusty seat backs.

"Here you are," he says, tipping my chin. His kiss reaches all the way down to the filth-littered floor below me, reminding me of my lack of control.

Jack nods to his foreman and points to the lobby as he leads me there. My hand feels small in his.

"I went with Nell to the hotel," I say.

"Has great potential, right?" He hides a smile by biting the inside of his lip.

"Did you know she wants to recruit me to be the director?"

"Sort of … I told her you'd do a great job."

"Before you and Nell plan out the rest of my life, I'd appreciate being in the loop."

"You're right. I'm sorry. She's my godmother and always butting into my problems."

"I'm a problem?"

"Let's back up and start over. Hello, Hope. How have you been? Did you get Micah and Dula settled?"

Taking a deep breath, I start pacing.   "The drive up was uneventful. Micah played games on his phone, and Dula was very nervous."

"In other words, she babbled?"

"When we pulled through the gate, they were so excited

that Micah jumped out of the car, dragging Dula with him. I had to hunt them down to say goodbye."

"Those were the days," Jack says wistfully.

"I take it you were a camper there?"

"Eight years a camper, three years a wrangler." He looks through the doorway to see if we are being watched before lifting me off the ground. "I've missed you so much." His voice is a husky whisper. Before letting me go, he buries his face in my hair, inhaling deeply. "You smell delicious."

I laugh. "If you don't stop these shenanigans, I might latch onto your lips and never let go."

"Shenanigans? You sound like mi abuela."

"I'm probably starting to look her age too. That hotel is hot and filthy." I fluff my hair.

"But you have such a gift for dealing with garbage."

"You did *not* just say that." I start chasing him.

"Wait, ouch! Stop pinching! You're such a girl!" Jack lets me catch him, and we lean together for a moment before he nibbles my ear. "Where do you want to eat tonight, your place?"

"I'm afraid to be alone with you," I say, pulling back.

"Don't you trust me? We've been together over a month."

"Maybe I don't trust myself."

"What do you mean?"

"I don't know what I mean," I say, wiggling out of his arms.

Like lightning, Jack's demeanor shifts, and he shoves his hands in his pockets. "Are you having second thoughts about us? Just tell me now, before ..." I see his jaw flex beneath his skin as he squints and looks out the door.

"Did you always date 'nice' girls?" I ask.

"That's a random question." The crease between his eyebrows deepens.

"I've been feeling squirrely and weird," I say, crossing my

arms and fighting the urge to resume pacing. "Let's just change the subject. How are the renovations coming?"

"I don't want to talk about the damn renovations. I want to talk about us. Why ask about my dating history?"

"Okay, I saw this woman today through the window of the Cactus Café. She had a kid that she loved, and it reminded me how damaged I am."

"Must have been Heidi Dunn and her son Russell."

"You know her? How well?"

"Yes, Hope, I know lots of people in this town. She's married to Charlie, my oldest friend. He's a cop, like Heidi's father."

"Jacob Lindheimer?"

"How do you know Jake?"

"Busy morning. I didn't mean to insinuate that every woman you know is an ex-girlfriend."

"Well, in the spirit of total honesty, we did have a thing one spring break when I was in college—before she and Charlie got together."

"A thing?"

Jack leans back against the candy counter. My head aches.

"The truth is, Hope, you and I both have battered pasts. I've done a million things I'm ashamed of ... broken laws, slept with women." He stares at his work boots. "I haven't been serious about anyone in years—and never while sober."

"Me neither." My voice sounds weak.

"I was doing fine, hiding out on the ranch, working my ass off building something, and then you showed up, all tormented and shiny."

"Shiny?" I ask.

"Don't ask me to explain. Combine that with the fact that you understand about addiction and love Micah and Dula ... good Lord, you make me crazy." He smiles, but his brows are still furrowed.

"Could that be a good thing?"

"I guess … hope so," he says, trapping me in his arms again.

"I think Nell should celebrate the reopening of this theater by showing a week of romantic movies."

"Romantic movies? Don't you mean acceptable porn for lonely women?"

I hit his arm, hard.

"Man, that actually hurt!"

"Tell me a romantic movie you've seen."

"I don't watch chick flicks."

"You do watch movies, right? If not, I'm gone—history."

"James Bond is a romantic dude, right?"

"When was the last time you went to the theater?"

"I've been busy. I watch all the old seasons of *The Walking Dead* on Netflix. Does that count?"

"For your information, James Bond isn't a romantic. He's a chauvinistic sex addict, unable to commit"

"No way!"

"What are we going to do, Jack?" I lift his arm and place it around my shoulders like a warm sweater. "Your kisses make me want to throw up."

"Exactly what every man wants to hear …"

"I didn't mean it like that."

"I know what you meant."

"I'm scared of you—of what might happen, good or bad." I start to cry.

"Listen, I haven't done relationships the right way either."

"Is there a right way?"

"This doesn't mean we can't start now, create something new," he says, stroking my hair.

"But *how*? Am I supposed to cross my legs or move in with you?"

"I don't know," he says, running both hands through his hair. "Why does it matter what we do?"

"I've always shot the finger at people who judged me. Of course I was usually drunk. You should walk away from me before I mess up your life," I say, backing toward the front door. "I didn't realize I was so bad at this—awkward all the time and jealous of everyone. Something inside whispers that you're too good for me—someone I don't deserve." Tears sting my eyes.

"Me too, Hope." Seemingly without thinking, Jack pulls a neatly folded bandana out of his back pocket and hands it to me while he talks. "I'm not supposed to grab you and tear your clothes off? I can't even make you a pitcher of my killer margaritas."

"You want to tear my clothes off?" I say in a small voice.

"What do you think?"

"That's kinda hot."

"Stop it, Hope."

"We're screwed," I say, "or maybe not ..."

Jack looks into my eyes, and his face softens. "We just need to go slowly, one date at a time."

I forget about the bandana and wipe my face on his shirt, listening to the vibration of his voice inside his chest.

"Here's the deal. I have to go to a cattle sale in Santa Fe for the next few days. The universe brought us together for a reason, and we'll figure out what to do next. Trust me."

CHAPTER 8

No way am I walking back past the Cactus Café, I tell myself after leaving the theater. I can't avoid my sordid past, and neither can Jack, but now that I know he's been to bed with Heidi, how will I ever be able to eat blueberry pancakes there again? I told him that I want to think about some things and we could start chipping away at our issues when he returns from Santa Fe.

On the city pamphlet I picked up, I noticed a small church with a very old graveyard and historical marker two or three blocks over from Main Street. Maybe some of the Pettibones are buried there—a good excuse for a detour.

I'm not sure why I've reverted to such an adolescent way of dealing with my feelings—so embarrassing. Could it be true that when you get sober, you revert to the emotional age you were when you first started drinking? Stunted at thirteen. Terrific.

Reboot!

Oz-God! Could you be any more annoying?

Is that an invitation?

No! I guess we have more to talk about now …

As much or as little as you choose.

I'm too old for the single life.

You are not.

I can't handle dating.

Handle new relationships or just the lust part?

I didn't say that.

What about your questions?

What questions?

Nice try.

Dang! I thought we'd already had the sex talk.

Ahh, you've figured everything out, then? Okay, buh-bye!

Wait. Don't go. Why has this become such big deal for me? Anyway, doesn't most of life happen in the gray areas?

Some say that there are at least fifty shades of it.

Why does your opinion matter to me all of a sudden?

You downloaded the Source app. We're interfacing.

Scary.

Lust isn't just about sex.

I'm falling for Jack, which causes me to have really intense … feelings.

Unlike the desire to mate, lust extends beyond procreation.

How so?

It's more obsessive, an intense need for control—to have a person, a job, or even a chocolate malt right now, *no matter what the consequence.*

So lust is bad.

What were we discussing earlier?

Could you narrow that down a bit?

Think beyond the good-versus-bad aspect of your feelings.

Can I ask you something?

No.

Wait, what?

Just kidding. Nothing is off-limits with me.

You say you are an expression of something good, even holy, and yet seem okay with me questioning taboo subjects.

A new concept for you, eh?

I had no idea how limited my inner life has been. Talking with you whenever I want is crazy.

Are you calling me crazy?

No, but this is so personal—goes against the groupthink I've associated with religion. That's one of the main reasons I pulled away from all of that. I don't trust words.

Religious words?

Actually, all words.

And yet you're so good with them.

Sometimes it feels as if words have been hijacked by dark forces that systematically strip them of any good vibe they used to have.

See what I mean? That statement is a very good assessment. When people lie or lose integrity and refuse to take responsibility for what they say, the frequency or true meaning can become imprisoned by doubt.

I've become cynical and manipulative with my words.

Manipulative?

Living a lie, hiding my past, investing everything into achievement and the image I projected as a strong woman and intelligent college professor … crock-o-shit.

Evolution takes time … Slow down a bit and savor the sewer gas. It's all fertilizer.

That's just warped. Besides, I need to know what to do right now!

Lusting for the answers?

So?

What have you been searching for, Hope?

To be loved, cherished—set apart as special.

By a man?

Not just a man.

Who else matters to you?

"Nell … maybe my brother Ronny."

Nell matters, so you agreed to clean the hotel when you didn't want to. Why?

So she will like me—give me a pat on the head.

After she says, 'Good girl,' what then?

Your point?

What if she starts taking advantage of you—hurts your feelings?

I'd be pissed.

Bad, bad Nell! See how easy it is to remain in good/bad duality? You don't even have to go to church to feed the habit.

I'm just trying to do the right thing for once. Are you telling me to ignore it when someone needs me or asks for a favor?

No, but human nature is flawed by design. Giving anyone else the power to define your worth is a setup for failure.

I don't know any other way.

Can you imagine a different response when someone hurts or offends you?

Other than self-righteous indignation?

Time to evolve, but only if you want to.

Do I have what it takes? I want this thing with Jack to work.

Will you look at what's under the lust?

I'm afraid that my heart's desire is something no man is capable of giving me.

CHAPTER 9

My feet are sweating inside tennis shoes that feel like lead pounding the blistering sidewalk. This side of town is quaint; the houses are old and a bit less ostentatious. Most intelligent inhabitants of Cypress Bend are sipping sweet tea inside while the asphalt shimmers like a mirage in the bald heat of July.

I see the thick, gnarled pecan trees like oversized sentinels on each side of a surprisingly small square building. Built of hand-hewn stone, the Methodist church features three arched windows on each side and a simple wooden entry door with bands and bolts of pocked and black-painted iron across it. Above the apex of the entrance is a small bell tower made of cypress planks that look to have been recently replaced.

There is indeed a historical marker stating that this was the town's first church, built around 1877—often referred to as "Annabelle's Chapel." For some reason, I feel a physical aversion to going inside. Maybe it's just the heat baking my brain.

The graveyard encompasses the sides and back of the churchyard, separated from the rest of the world by a spike-tipped wrought-iron fence. The gate is stiff and further impaired by an overgrowth of grass. Why didn't I eat lunch?

My mouth is dry, and I feel as wobbly as some of the tilting headstones. I push through, seeking shade.

There is something so squishy about the dirt in a grave-yard, as if the coffins with their bodies trapped inside have rotted and the lost souls want to suck me down to keep them company. I whisper the names carved into the stones as I weave among them. Some epitaphs are so worn that they've become erased, the memories forever muted.

I can't escape the startling reminder—all these people were once living and breathing, as real as I am. Their pain and fear seem to rise from the moist earth like a mist of remembrance, mixing with my own past. Do I have a graveyard somewhere inside of me where I've covered up dead or unloved parts of myself? And are my ex-lovers buried alive and still screaming? If I trespass there, will I fall into a pit of my own making?

At the far back corner of the cemetery is another gate leading out into what might have been a church garden. There is a carved, lichen-covered bench where I immediately sit, and then lie down, resting my sweaty cheek against the cool marble. Overhead, dappled light filters through the leaves of another huge pecan tree, and the mind-altering surge of heat inside me slowly subsides.

From my sideways position, I can see the ground around the bench. A few feet to my right is a rectangular headstone lying flush with the ground and partially concealed by pink-flowered vinca plants. I gently push the pretty leaves aside and read the epitaph: "Annabelle Pettibone—born March 1, 1893, died June 7, 1909." Carved in smaller letters at the bottom are the words "Baby Pettibone."

"What the hell?" I sit up too fast and see black sparkles for a moment. I'm surprised by the grief choking me. Why are this poor seventeen-year-old girl and her baby buried outside of hallowed ground? She was a Pettibone, for God's sake. What happened—did her family shun her? Did she die in childbirth? This poor girl could have been me in a time before birth control.

Stinging tears burn trails down my face, and my heart breaks a little more. What's happening to me?

CHAPTER 10

Hope, where are yooouuu?

I'm in the bathtub nursing a headache under lavender-scented bubbles.

Why do you bathe in the dark?

I'm hiding, of course.

From me?

I don't like being naked—physically or mentally.

Yet you don't mind wearing a bikini on the beach?

I know ... even though I hate the way I look. Doesn't make sense.

Why don't you like your reflection?

Because I can't see what's really there, only exaggerated faults and imperfections. I feel ugly and fat all the time and can't accept compliments. How's that for defective wiring?

By any standard, you are a beautiful woman

And if I weren't?

All souls are created from the same Source.

Maybe I've learned how to dress up, wear makeup, and do my hair, but it doesn't change how I feel inside. I can walk down the beach half-naked because the real me is inside with invisible hands covering my face."

You've felt this way all your life?

Seems as if I was born ashamed. Can we inherit something like that?

On many levels.

I guess you saw me at the graveyard. It was as if I could hear the dead trying to describe their lives to me … somehow defending their behavior in life. It was really trippy, so I sat down on a bench under a pecan tree to catch my breath. Why am I telling you this? You were probably watching the whole thing.

Being aware and being invited are two different ways of being present.

Well, I basically flipped out, while obsessing over the poor girl buried outside the gate.

Annabelle Pettibone?

Who was she?

Why don't you ask Nell to tell you about her?

What, you can't talk about it? Do you have some type of spirit–human confidentiality clause?

Everything happens for a reason. Aren't you glad?

I see.

Tell me more.

For a few moments I almost *was* her, you know? Young and fresh, she walked with a man in a straw boater's hat and slacks with suspenders. I felt her joy and confidence, and then almost immediately, the picture darkened and fast-forwarded—she sat sobbing on what seemed like the same bench I was sitting on. She was pregnant and totally alone.

Same issues, different century.

Except she and her baby died. I suspect that the circumstances were terrible.

Tell me about when you were sixteen."

That was around the time when boys started doing the blush and shuffle around me. Suddenly, like Annabelle, I felt strong … at least for a date or two.

And later, when the stakes were higher?

Don't forget, I started out damaged.
Your relationships became intimate quickly?
I guess at some level, I didn't feel I had the right to say no.
Can we talk about something else now?
Did a man ever look behind your attractive exterior?
The getting-to-know-you part was never high on the agenda. I thought maybe when I got married, there would be enough time to go deeper. Wrong. Once Steve owned me, he lost interest.
Was it high on your *agenda?*
What do you mean?
Emotional intimacy—you know, getting to know your husband, or any man you dated, at a deeper level?
I hate it when you do that.
To what are you referring, pray tell?
Turning the tables.
Lust can be a two-way street.
Okay, so my man-picker is broken. I'm attracted to good-looking and emotionally unavailable men so I can blame them when the relationship collapses. Is that what you want to hear?
Your fingers and toes are pickled.
I'm getting out of the tub. Don't look.
I was at the quilting bee in your mother's womb.
What?
You know, when your body was pieced together.
Talk about invasive.
I'm not some sort of Peeping Tom trying to catch you naked or picking your nose.
Where do you go when we aren't talking?
Nowhere, just look in the mirror.
But I hate mirrors!
If you hate yourself, how can you love anyone else?
I semi-trust you.

Baby steps …

Do you see everything, *all* the time?

Nothing is hidden in the higher dimensions. However, if it makes you feel better, we most often perceive you as light, not body parts.

Still creepy.

To be known at a pre-atomic level.

My thoughts are unacceptable and sometimes dark and dirty, and I don't want you to see them!

Unacceptable to whom?

That's an interesting question.

Would you have killed your childhood puppy for rummaging in the garbage can?

No, but I might have spanked the crap out of her.

Rummaging is in her nature.

Yes, and my own garbage smells *so* good … woof, woof.

Putting emotions on a leash can be difficult.

What is it with you and metaphors?

It's a habit I have.

So, Oz-God, do you hang around, you know, when people are doing it?

You cannot make me uncomfortable. I love your questions.

You aren't going to swat me with a newspaper?

I won't, but there may be others who are offended by your courage.

Should I stop asking?

Absolutely not.

The days of my silent victimhood seem to be shifting.

It's awesome to watch.

But I still think that men are wired differently from women—at least the ones I run into.

Is that a fact?

I'm probably the worst person to analyze men.

Just talk to me. You don't have to be politically correct. We are unraveling the unique story of your past, with all the warts.

Warts are ugly. The Wicked Witch of the West had warts, and look what happened to her.

What is attractive then?

In my father's eyes?

We can start with him.

His definition would be a woman in a tight, short dress and high heels with her boobs hanging out. I would bet money that he traded 'favors' with some of the prostitutes he arrested.

In other words, dress sexy, and men will want you, love you?

Don't most boys start out with the *Victoria's Secret* catalogue? Dad said if a girl goes out on the town looking like a hooker, then she probably wants guys to pick her up. I was a flat-chested kid and yet always felt that what he did to me was my fault. I was too young to look like a hooker, so why did he molest me?

I'm so sorry that happened to you. Your father was broken in many areas.

None of it makes sense. I'll admit, it's hard not to blame your kind for not stopping him even though I am getting a better understanding of the dark side of free will.

I hope you can forgive me someday.

Me forgive you?

If you blame me for something, then I'm no different from any other hurtful person in your life.

I never thought of it that way.

Your mother was a victim too.

I haven't really opened the Mom package yet. I hated her weakness, though, how she never defended us and cringed around my dad.

So you grew up believing that there are primitive wiring differences between the sexes and that women usually deserve whatever they get because they are weaker?

How can I admit to such an archaic misconception?

And yet here we are …

If I were a man, I would hate me. I tantalize and test them, basically demanding they do everything my way. One minute, I'm hot after a guy's body; the next, nonresponsive and crying for attention like a selfish little girl.

So you think that some women are victimizers too? I don't know. I'm all twisted up about it.

Don't worry; we're in the sorting phase of how your belief system was created.

But I am horrified that I've been disrespectful and sexist toward men. What woman does that? Especially these days?

As long as you're baring your soul …

I do have a bottom line, though. Nothing gives a man or a woman license to sexually assault anyone, even if she or he is walking down the street naked with a 'Come and Get It' sign.

Define your interpretation of assault.

Now there's a gray area. I suppose you're going to tell me I have to look deeper.

Now we're cooking—that is, if you're still hungry.

Don't get all excited.

Let me have my moment, okay?

CHAPTER 11

All night, the graves and their undead inhabitants infiltrate my dreams. With sticky, rotting fingers they tug at my secrets, their breath like toxic fumes creep under the door like a vaporous "come hither." I awaken midmorning, dripping with sweat.

The backyard of my cottage slopes down to the riverbank, where rough rock steps provide access to the dock. With my first cup of coffee, I sit on the back porch swing and watch the green ripples flowing by.

I'm finding it more and more difficult to doubt what is happening inside me, yet how can Oz-God be real? I've never heard of an unhaunted relationship with a spiritual entity. We've been interacting for over four months—first at the beach, then at the ranch, and now here. It doesn't feel like insanity.

Around front, I hear car tires crunching on gravel and then voices at my door. It's not Nell, so who? Ahh, it's Patty and Jake Lindheimer, and they're fighting. What are they doing here? I don't know them well enough for a visit. I just met them yesterday.

"You have to tell her, Jacob. Jack can't—he's out of town!" Patty's voice is set on scold mode.

"The only thing I *have* to do is pay taxes and die!" he fires back.

"You better do what I say if you want to eat again."

I cover my mouth to keep from laughing. I should walk around and greet them, but they haven't knocked on the door yet, and I might miss their impromptu performance.

The chief continues. "Come to think of it, I don't have to pay taxes *or* mind you. I could tell Portnoy to lock you in a cell where I wouldn't have to listen to your yammering day and night."

"I'd like to see Deputy Doofus try to touch me," she snorts.

Their repartee feels like country dancing—lots of swinging and posturing while moving in perfect rhythm.

"Knock on the door, you old coot. This is important. Her car is here. Maybe she—"

My stomach feels heavy and rolls over. "Hello? Hello! I'm on the back porch, guys!" I yell. My legs don't want to move. What if something has happened to the kids?

Patty comes around the corner carrying a pie with golden, crisscrossed crust on top. I feel sick. Grabbing my stomach with both hands, I fold in half.

"Hey, sweetie, are you okay?" Jacob clomps up the steps and puts his big hand on my back.

Assessing the situation, Patty moves quickly. She sets the pie on the porch and disappears into the house, returning with a glass of water. "I guess you aren't used to surprise visitors," she says, her voice clipped with something I suspect is actually shyness. "Don't worry," she continues. "It's not bad news, if that's what you're frettin' about."

Looking up, I see her widen her eyes at her husband, motioning a "go ahead" message with her head.

The big man sighs. "Actually, our news is good, I think. Jack wanted to surprise you. I'll be damned if the 'system' didn't work in our favor for once."

Patty wipes her hands on the front of her dress where a work apron is usually tied. "It's about your brother, Hope. That's why we're here."

"*My* brother? Ronny? I haven't talked to him in over two years. How do you know ... What's ... Is he dead?"

"No!" Jacob exclaims. "No, he isn't dead at all. In fact, he's coming here, to Cypress Bend, any day."

"Wait, what do you mean? I thought he was in a mental hospital?" My head is spinning.

Jacob looks at Patty, and she fidgets. "I told you boys to talk to her first. Always gotta meddle ..." Her straight-line mouth is back.

"Dang it, I wish Jack was here to tell you the details." Jacob looks at the ground. "Your brother's been living on his own for over a year, taking college classes, I think. Someone at social services helped him track you to the World's End ranch—made some arrangement with Jack for a visit. Guess we should have checked with you." Jacob stops talking when he sees my frozen look.

Patty takes my arm in case I faint. "Come here and sit on the swing."

"Ronny is coming here? When?"

"Soon is all I heard," says Jacob. "Could be today or next week. Just thought you'd wanna know about it beforehand."

"I guess this isn't such good news after all?" Patty asks.

"What? No, uh ... yes. It's kind of a miracle that Ronny is better ... can make it on his own."

"If he comes while Jack is out of town, he can stay at the police station and sleep on my couch or in one of the unoccupied ... cots."

"Have you lost your mind?" Patty puts her fists on her hips and glares at her husband. "Put this poor girl's brother in a cell after all that time he spent in an institution? It's you who's gonna be sleeping on that cot, old man."

"Okay, you're right. I wasn't thinking. I'll put your brother up at the hotel where Jack has a room—give you two some time to get reacquainted?"

"Come on, Jacob. Let's give the poor girl some space." Patty hands me the pie. "Sorry, hon. Eat this. It might help."

CHAPTER 12

Why am I afraid of the "Bone" Hotel? Broken chairs and dirty windows are tangible items to check off my list, not like my other worries. Ronny is coming here? I don't think I'm up for what might slither to the surface. What if our repressed histories have mutated into a new weapon of mass destruction?

Are you afraid of hurting him?

And myself. Is that selfish or what?

No, it's healthy. The only one standing in judgment of your reaction is you.

Maybe so, but here in the real world, there's a shit-pot full of people waiting for me to fail.

Who?

I don't know ... just *them*!

One cage of rabid squirrels at a time, Hope. Think fertilizer.

All I know to do is approach each room in the hotel as I would one more day of sobriety. Windex, sponges, and trash bags ... work like a dog, and then tonight, put my feet up with a Diet Coke and call to scold Jack for not telling me about Ronny.

Hope, look out!

Ouch! Crap! Stop distracting me! You made me fall off the

curb right in front of the hotel. Now my knee is bleeding, and my phone has a crack across the front.

I warned you.

Oh, look, there's more. See how someone has spray-painted a skull with crossbones, on the sign that Nell put up yesterday? Wow. My day is already packed with good omens, not.

Cast out the deeemons!

Like I would know anything about that.

No, really. Pay attention to everything happening right now.

I'm bleeding. Don't you care about that? What if I decided that the planets have aligned against me and painted skulls, and a broken phone mean impending cosmic disaster?

You say 'tomato,' and I say gird your loins.

You're being … stranger than usual.

Did you notice how the front door creaks?

Quit messing with me. There better be something good about this nightmare job.

You're blessed.

Why do you say that?

Not everyone who cleans out the cat box expects buried treasure.

Yeah, cat turds, that's about right.

Many of the Pettibone old-timers say this hotel has ghosts.

Takes one to know one.

Did you hear that?

Nope, not falling for it. Out of my way. I'm going to march into every one of these rooms and take notes about what needs to be done. Devil be damned!

The last door on the left … bwahaha!

I'm ignoring you.

I'm used to it.

Ronny would love this old place.

Tell me about him.

Not sure I want to dig around for those memories right now.

Where are they?

On some major guilt planet in another galaxy.

Why guilt?

What happened to him was my fault.

That's how you see it?

I don't want to talk to you any more. Won't you let me do something mindless for once?

Self-torture takes a lot of energy.

Gee … how did I ever survive without you?

If you described your brother to a stranger, what would you say?

He is beautiful, creative, and … fragile. He's also gay and has suffered greatly. I don't know what he's like now.

It's been two years?

Since I spoke with him. Seven since he was attacked.

Explain to me why this is your fault.

I had just started at the university and a few of my gay friends seemed open and at ease with their orientation. I encouraged Ronny to get honest and come out.

Honesty can be a good thing.

Not in our family. When Ronny told our father, the roof blew off. My dad screamed that he had sullied the Delaney name and deserved a public beating.

Still not your fault.

Betraying him was the worst thing I could have done! I tossed my baby brother into the jaws of the monster, who kicked him out of the house. The next time I saw Ronny was in the hospital, all broken, crazy-bloody, and just … absent. I wanted to kill myself.

It wasn't your father who beat him?

Does emotional slaughter count?

What did your mother do?

Some nosy neighbors brought food and told my mom that Ronny had the dark spirit of homosexuality attached to him and they wanted to pray it out of him.

No one was charged for the assault?

We suspected Ronny knew the boys who beat him up, but he wouldn't tell. He just checked out mentally. I couldn't stand it, so I cut off contact and locked any door labeled 'Family.'

Knock, knock.

Go away.

CHAPTER 13

For once, I'm not hugging the toilet because I'm drunk. Between bouts of vomiting and urgent evacuation from the other end, I contemplate the terrifying effectiveness of the common stomach bug. When the phone rings, I fumble with it twice before I can answer.

"How's my favorite workhorse?" Nell sounds so chipper I may have to purge again.

"Frankly, I don't have the energy to recite my litany of woes. I've either been poisoned by my breakfast taco, or invaded by a stomach virus."

"Poor baby. I'm in San Antonio but I could call Patty Lindheimer and see if she could send over some soup."

My guts grind at the thought of food. "No, don't bother her. She and Jacob have alreaky been too nice. They brought me a pie the other day when they gave me the news about Ronny."

"Now, Ronny is …"

"Didn't I tell you about my brother?"

"Isn't he in a mental health facility?"

"Yes, and evidently, he has been out on his own for over a year, taking classes and everything."

"That's good news, right?"

"Yes … and no. He is coming to visit me here, in Cypress Bend, any day now. I haven't seen him in seven years."

"Ahh, that explains the vomiting."

"Don't start. Are you inferring that this horrible virus is all in my mind?" I feel a wave of dizziness ripple through me and move to the bathroom and sit on the side of the bathtub just in case.

"You, of all people, should embrace the idea that the stomach is like an emotional brain."

"Listen, Nell, that brain is telling me to end this call and go lie down. I'll call you tomorrow, okay?"

"Just let me know about Patty and the soup. I'm sure she won't mind. I'll be praying for a quick recovery."

"Okay, bye." I wonder if Patty knows about Nell and her husband's teenage love story? If Nell asks Patty for soup, she might just spit in it. I close my eyes and chuckle.

Hope, are you feeling better?

For the love of God, what are you waking me up for?

Do you believe in miraculous healing?

Since you didn't bless me with any, I don't think I need to answer that question. Your timing is terrible.

Really? From my vantage point, your innards look perfect to me. Try thinking about eating crisp, cold watermelon on a summer day. That might distract you and make my presence less nauseating.

I love watermelon and, I do feel better after a nap. Why are you asking me about healing?

I just want to know your thoughts.

You already know my thoughts.

Yes, in some higher dimensional way, but …

You are just 'guiding' me toward a certain conversation you want to have, right?

Actually, questions about sickness and miraculous healing escaped from your mind while you were sleeping.

I suppose that 'razzle-dazzle' healing could be possible at some quantum level, but Iyou know I don't have faith in magical thinking.

Of course you don't.

For example, say someone 'gets healed' and his or her cancerous tumors disappear. A year or so later, the tumors come back, worse than before. What's miraculous about that?

No one, not even spontaneously healed people, escapes the process of looking for the reasons for imbalance..

So, I suspect there must be something in us like 'cancerous thinking?' I've said before, my neuropsychology teacher convinced me that thoughts are chemicals. I guess you can cut out a cancer, but if the toxic thoughts don't change ...

Processing is a choice.

Speaking of Ronny and me ...

Does Ronny have cancer?

Do I?

What were you saying about the two of you?

I don't understand why so much fear and condemnation surround some issues and not others.

Issues?

You know, mistakes, royal fuck ups ... most people call them sins.

Sin is sin. In Spanish sin means, without.

Without what?

Without connection to the Source.

There is so much fighting about what's a big sin, a little one, visible or hidden. And what about the bad stuff that everyone does, so somehow, it's okay?

Sin Gumbo.

I can cook.

For someone who claims she isn't religious, you know quite a few of the ingredients contained in condemnation.

When some horrible event happens in the world, like a

politician runs off with all the pension money or a priest has an affair or molests an altar boy, there is shock and awe, and a new wave of black-and-white hatred begins.

So many societal topics are reaching a fever pitch, some, which mirror the internal conflicts that individuals like you are experiencing.

Sometimes the future feels hopeless.

What would you suggest we do about it?

I have no power to cause change at that level.

Didn't you say once, in a cannabis moment, that you could see the whole world on your fingernail?

Yes, I'm guilty of a few dope-smoking clichés.

What if it's true?

I need to do the dishes.

Go ahead. Do you think Jack is different from the other men you've been with?

He has to be. I no longer believe in coincidences.

What else do you believe?

You're pissing me off and I want a donut.

Why don't you ask the question pinging around in your brain?

I've been sick, leave me alone!

Yes, but you vomited through a doorway to your feelings and I'm capitalizing on the moment.

You are so warped.

Just speaking your language.

Fine. Jack and I are struggling with how to move forward. I guess that's obvious.

Neither of you is new to the relationship game.

Sometimes I wish I were asexual.

Sex was created not to be a nightmare but to be a little bit of heaven to make multiplying a most enjoyable event.

Can you please stop?

I've waited a long time to talk about this.

With me?

Not just you.

Fine, let the torture begin.

Oh my, you are stressed.

AA beliefs are messing with my head.

How so?

My sponsor wanted me to abstain from sex for three to six months. So stupid! I got divorced four months ago!

How long since your last relapse, two months?

I don't think I believe in marriage any more. Can't I have a deep, fulfilling relationship without 'forever' looming over my head?

Jack makes you think about marriage?

Maybe it's the lust you were talking about before.

Only lust?

Yes … no … maybe lust plus something else that makes me even more nervous.

Romance is an art form.

Just peachy for all the poets and creative types, but what about the rest of us?

What's your perception of intimacy?

Sex is everywhere—it's more like bowling or yoga. These days, using a website to hook up is about as available and intimate as beer pong. Internet porn may seem safe but it can lead to isolation and a different sort of misery. I think desensitization has caused intimacy to lose meaning.

What have you done with Hope Delaney?

I'm not a total moron.

You don't see much difference between intimacy and sex.

I just thought—

What about humor, deep friendship, and familiarity?

I give up. I have no idea how to approach this subject, especially with you.

What would you tell your sixteen-year-old daughter about sex?

What a dreadful scenario to contemplate.

Pretend.

If I had a daughter, I would probably scare her to death with tales of disease and unwanted pregnancy, interlaced with painful vignettes of abuse from my sordid past and, maybe a bit of hell fire.

Why would you do that?

Family tradition?

Aren't those the very concepts you rebelled against?

How else could I protect my daughter from making the same mistakes I did? I know I sound hypocritical, but you put me on the spot.

There are countless ways to approach the subject.

This is horrifying. I can't have a constructive conversation about sexuality with anyone.

Why?

I haven't figured it out myself.

Sex is a sticky wicket.

Eww, don't say sticky.

Then you don't really have a philosophy of sex.

I've gathered random bits of religious guilt and parental shame, mixed it with a so-called enlightened attitude toward sexual freedom, and finished the toxic cocktail with a splash of self-righteous justification for my irresponsible behavior. I have nothing healthy to give Jack, much less pass on to any children.

There is so much more to your story.

No fair! You know all the answers about my future but won't tell me what to do.

Telling you what to do isn't my job, remember?

I'm miserable and have to clean up this nasty building all summer. Thanks a whole freaking lot! Oh, and before my adrenaline recedes or I drop dead from a lightning bolt; let me say for the record that two hormone-pumped teenagers should never get married just to have sex. Their brains are barely mylenated and, they don't know who they are or what they want in life—beyond having a sports car or killer prom dress.

Good point, in most cases.

None of the boys I knew back then thought for one nanosecond about fatherhood or being a good provider and responsible life partner.

Having a baby at that age can hijack your life—present a different set of lessons.

Is that a good or bad thing?

Let's experiment.

In what way?

If we step out of black-and-white thinking, what is teen pregnancy?

Remove the traditional judgment on the issue?

What were you looking for when you experimented with sex?

I wanted a way to escape my home life … my father. I wanted to feel special, damn it, for some young hero to vanquish the dragon and free me from my tower of terror.

Not necessarily a strong foundation for eternal love but a choice you made based on your experiences.

I know you're trying to teach me something, but I still don't get it.

There are consequences to every decision you make, some of them beyond your control.

Yeah, either we are blessed, or we burn in hell.

No.

What do you mean, no?

No, that isn't how this works.

I'm all ears.

Relationship with me isn't about judging; it's about processing every single thought, action, and consequence that happens through a love you can't destroy.

Even if Jack and I have sex?

We are processing the hell out of this subject.

You're not supposed to cuss.

I mean it literally. When we do this together, hell and all its minions flee.

Metaphorically speaking.

In all dimensions and through all belief systems.

The real problem is that sex feels good. You have an immediate, tangible connection to someone who wants to be with you—even if it's for an hour with no strings attached.

Oxytocin can become addictive.

What's oxytocin?

A hormone released during sex that is supposed to help build and maintain feelings of deep bonding and trust.

Not much use on a one-night stand.

Sex with no meaning can cause emptiness and depression.

So basically, you're saying that a chemical created to build relationships becomes just another drug I can use to fix my feelings?

And in a young and naive person, the chemical euphoria can be mistaken for true love.

Romeo and Juliet syndrome.

The classic illustration.

I can understand the argument for encouraging young people to wait, but wait for what, exactly?"

In my dimension every type of being can see you, watch your behavior. When you think about the unseen world, who do most people imagine?

Are you trying to scare me?

Where do you think the concept of Satan and his demons came from?

I believe in evil, but not with a pitchfork.

Who do you think tortures you in the night, reminding you of your shameful past, whispering lies that you are ruined and can never be forgiven?

So evil, however I define it becomes a tortuous being

off-roading around my map of negative neural pathways of anger and shame?

Without permission.

What have you done with nice, funny Oz-God?

Spiritual DNA activation is a serious job sometimes.

I can't wait to see how you're going to relate all this to sex.

Intimacy is about respect—for yourself and the other person.

So there's hope? No, don't say it ...

Making love was created to be the French silk pie at the end of a banquet of getting to know each other, building trust, and commitment.

Sounds delicious.

CHAPTER 14

Crack!

Lightning flashes, and marble-sized hail pelts the window. I sit up so fast that my stomach muscles cramp. Unwinding from the sheets, I hurry to the bathroom and wrap a fleece robe around my chilled body.

With the storm slamming against the house, I have no desire for more sleep. Community Coffee with chicory, served in a cup with puppies and kitties on it—that's the ticket.

Maybe demons are real. Where did that come from? Oh yes, I was dreaming that Satan had moved into my college apartment. My mother and I were trying to make the king-sized bed in my room, but the sheets were dirty and too small, and the patterns didn't match. My mom kept saying, "Shh!" Not a very subtle dream interpretation.

The wind flings a branch against the front door, making me jump and almost spill my coffee. Since my recent experience with a tornado at the ranch, storms have felt more threatening. I breathe deeply, willing myself to relax. I miss Jack. He comes home from Santa Fe tomorrow. I smile and then frown.

Another branch hits the door, then another, until I realize something is pounding—a person, I hope. "God in heaven, protect me …" My whisper sounds weak, not like anything that would stop a demon.

Through the peephole I see a woman, wet and small and wearing an oversized sweatshirt. After I unlock the deadbolt, she trips over the threshold.

"Are you okay? Is someone chasing you?" I relock the door and take off my robe, wrapping it around her shoulders. She could be a murderer, and I might be the dumbest person ever. "Wait here, I'll get you some towels."

She nods, sob-gasping.

Somewhere between the front door and the bathroom, I realize that the woman is the waitress I saw with Patty at the Cactus Café, Heidi Dunn—Jack's old girlfriend. She's no demon, only a fellow drunk stumbling around on a stormy night.

"Take this towel. Your hair is dripping. Should I call someone? Your father, maybe?" I feel helpless.

Heidi stiffens and recoils from my hand, as if remembering something. She sways and breathes heavily through her mouth, trying to focus. The smell of tequila fills the room, and her eyes dart around as if she is scoping out the nearest place to throw up.

"Hey, let's go in the bathroom for a sec, okay?" I say gently.

"I'm not sick. I don't need any help!"

"I know. I just thought a cold washcloth might—"

Heidi covers her mouth and runs, barely making it to the toilet. When I see she isn't bleeding or dying, I shut the door and get another coffee cup. Must be something serious to make her run out on a night like this without a car or raincoat. I check my phone to see if I have service. *Breathe.*

Heidi emerges a few minutes later, shaky but less panicked. "I used your hairbrush. Sorry, I shouldn't have. I can't believe I just used your brush like we're friends or something."

"No problem. I have some dry clothes too. Want some coffee?"

"Yes, lots of cream. My stomach …" Heidi collapses on

the couch. "I should go. I'm mortified. I can barely remember leaving the bar. I never go to bars!"

"I used to go to bars every night," I say, eager to ease her embarrassment.

Heidi nods, her upper body swaying slightly. "This guy ... he kept buying me shots. I didn't care. Just kept pounding them down ... Then I had to go pee, and all of a sudden, I'm running here ... in the lightning."

"Listen, let's start over. I'm Hope Delaney, which you probably know. You're Heidi, right? I've met your parents—nice folks. Your mom made me the most amazing pie."

"I made that pie."

As she looks at me, I wonder if she spit in it.

She sinks further into the couch and sighs. "Yeah, my parents are okay. Always strict as hell, but they love me. I've tried to make everybody happy—be a good wife and mother. My son is always in trouble, hanging with the wrong crowd. Daddy picked them up at the quarry the other day, doing God knows what. I don't even *want* to know anymore."

Heidi sets her coffee cup on the table with shaky hands and lies down on her back, probably to make the room stop spinning. "I heard Jack was back in town. When I saw you staring at me through the café window ... I don't know. The bottom just dropped out of everything. Jack's in love with you, and I'm just a stupid waitress with a delinquent child and a husband who—"

"I had no idea you and Jack were so close. He said it was more like a one-time fling."

She shakes her head. "He never knew how I felt, not *any* of it."

"Are you sure you don't want me to call your husband? I'm sure he's worried."

Heidi may need to vent, but her stagger down memory lane is giving me chills—not the good kind.

"How do *you* know Charlie? Are you buddies with him too?" Her shift toward nasty is swift.

"No, I've never met him. I do know he is Jack's best friend."

"*Was* his best friend. Nobody knows anything, don't you *see*? Have you got something stronger than coffee to drink?"

"Why don't you tell me why you came here? You made quite an effort."

"Jack used to stay in this cottage, you know? He knew where the spare key was. It was his special place … during holidays." She smiles and then hides her face before continuing. "Charlie wants to send Russell to military school—just like a cop, right? Beat it out of the kid!"

"Is your husband abusing Russell?" I ask.

"You mean hitting? No, he wouldn't dare." Heidi gets up and begins pacing, trying not to weave. She stops and cocks her head, listening. The rain is still falling, but the thunder and lightning have quieted. In the distance I hear a police siren.

"Shit," she says, and resignation settles on her face like cement. "I've never told anyone this—not even my husband or parents."

The police car pulls in front of the cottage, no siren now, only blue and red flashing lights in the windows. Suddenly, I know what she is going to say and grip my hands together.

"I don't know how to tell Jack that Russell is his son."

CHAPTER 15

The sun is up, just barely. Someone at the bar saw Heidi leave in the rain without her purse and called her husband. Small town. Charlie tracked his wife to my cottage. Maybe he knows more than Heidi thinks.

After a stiff and embarrassing exchange with Charlie and a tormented look from Heidi, I close the door, pick up the wet towels and dispose of Heidi's soggy Kleenexes. If only I could tidy up her looming secret that easily.

Obviously, Jack doesn't know about the child. Didn't he ever suspect? Guys can be so dumb. He said it was a one-night stand, but was it? My mind won't stop churning. I pace and mumble as if possessed.

Why did she decide to spill the beans now—and to me? Is she jealous and looking to make sure Jack and I don't stay together? What if Heidi is thinking of leaving her husband and—

Let's play the 'what scares Hope the most?' game.

Russell is going to change everything. There is no way to predict how Jack will react to having a son. Maybe Heidi will look different to him now. What if Charlie finds out and goes after Jack with his service revolver?

Slow down.

And who knows what that boy may do? He's already rebelling—he'll probably hate all of us and run away. I would.

Nice disaster plans. Are you thinking about joining him?

I *know* about adolescent angst. Preparing for the worst means surviving the present.

Suppressed lies eventually rise to the surface in one form or another.

Are you saying that Russell is acting out his mother's secret?

Some children do.

Even if they don't know what the secret is?

Actually, this could be a healing moment for everyone—a blessing in disguise.

Even if I lose Jack?

Aren't you tired of living with lies?

I'm overloaded. I need to stop analyzing every damn thing—just clean and sweep, pick up heavy things, and shove them down the stairs! Nell is right. Every thought in my head is crap.

I don't remember her saying that.

Look around me—there is crap on these porches, burnt crap everywhere, rat crap, and crap I can smell but not identify!

Okay, so today, art mimics life.

Thanks, Andy Warhol.

What if Woody Allen were directing your life-movie?

I'd be having much more fun. You would play the local rabbi. The Cactus Café would be full of townspeople and their relatives eating kosher food and offering opinions about Jack, Heidi, and me—all at the same time. Our sins and neuroses would be exposed loudly with much sarcasm and passive-aggressive advice.

Mazel tov! I am there, with popcorn.

CHAPTER 16

"I'd stop before you get to the china. Nell has a thing about family heirlooms."

Jack stands in the archway of the hotel kitchen with his hands over his ears, watching me throw Coke bottles in the direction of a fifty-five-gallon drum.

"Jack!" I toss the last bottle and jump at him. "I missed you so much. You smell like new truck seat leather."

"And you smell like sweet sweat and cleaning products."

"How long have you been watching me?" I ask, kicking at a Coke bottle that is rolling away from my frenzy.

"Long enough to see about fifty poltergeists pack up their chains and hightail it outta here. You're kinda scary ... and really loud."

"Well, I was, uh ... sorting stuff. It feels great to smash glass. Wanna try?"

"All of this destructive *enthusiasm* wouldn't have anything to do with Heidi's visit last night, would it?" he asks.

My Playtex Living Gloves make a loud rubbery snap when I take them off. "Who told you?" I ask, trying to wind my hair into an even tighter bun.

Jack watches me in a calm, annoying way, probably trying to read my body language. "Tell me what happened."

"Heidi was okay, just drunk. Yes, it was awkward. She appears like a wet dog at my door in the middle of the night, throws up, and starts rambling. I don't think her home life is too peachy right now."

"Probably Russell ..." Jack's face softens. "Charlie was a mess, and now his son is returning the favor."

"It wasn't that big of a deal."

"What else happened?"

"Nothing."

"No feelings at all?"

"Oh, those! Do you mean like how confused I am about your relationship with her, how angry she got about this and that, or how much fun it was to clean up her vomit?"

"I'm sorry that happened. I'll have to find out what's been going on with them."

"I don't care if you see her."

"Hope, you and I are like wounded animals trying to trust each other. Heidi, Charlie, and I share so many childhood memories."

"And don't forget, one very adult holiday," I add.

"Obviously, that night didn't mean much to her either. Within two months, she was married to Charlie." Jack shakes his head.

Didn't he think that was strange? "I get it, Jack. I really do."

Jack looks out the kitchen window. "Sometimes I feel so heavy, forced to drag the dead bodies of past girlfriends behind me forever."

"It's interesting how concerned you are about understanding Heidi's issues from the past, but you didn't find it necessary to discuss Ronny's visit with me. Did it occur to you that I might have something to say about that messed-up situation?" Without thinking I pick up a wooden spoon.

He shakes his head. "I thought it would be a nice surprise, but I should've known it would be a loaded subject for you."

"For me? So I'm the only one with family problems?"

"I didn't mean it that way," Jack says, his frustration rising.

"Ronny is *my* brother."

"Fine. Once again, I missed the big picture, trying to be your hero. What do you want me to do—cancel everything, tell him you don't want him to come?"

I burst into tears. "I hate surprises! I'm so nervous to see him after all this time."

"Don't cry … I'm not used to thinking about someone else's feelings."

"Well, you better start!"

"Don't threaten me. I'll try, okay?"

I stand very still, trying not to react to his reprimand.

Jack takes a slow, deep breath, and when he speaks again, his voice sounds less defensive. "Were you ever planning on making amends to Ronny? He is basically your only family."

I feel more tears spill out of my eyes, but I can't speak, and Jack continues.

"When he and I spoke on the phone, he shared some of what happened to him and said he really misses you. I think he was crying."

"Yeah, he cries. What did he tell you?" I ask.

"He can share that with you if he wants to. Now are you going to spank me with that spoon or what?"

"This spoon?" I lift it in a menacing way. "I once saw Nell swat a grown man with one of these. It looked like fun."

"I have been a very bad boy …"

I look from his sulky face to the spoon in my hand and start laughing and fling it at him. "Is this what is supposed to happen?" I cough and try to catch my breath.

"Laughter after anger?" Jack's slight head cock and cocker spaniel look send me off into more wheezing.

"No! No, *this*, talking about stuff instead of ignoring and resenting each other for a week or two. Never mind. That was a dumb question. Of course, this is what should happen."

We both calm down, and Jack hugs me.

"I don't think anyone has ever tried to be my hero before," I say.

"I'll help you get through this thing with Ronny, but now we need to practice enjoying our time together and trust God more."

My face freezes.

Jack squeezes his eyebrows together. "Too religious?" He seems nervous.

"I should feel weird, but I don't."

The sunset is gentle, a delicate blend of pink and purple stacking up on the horizon. Jack and I sit in rusted folding chairs behind the hotel, watching fireflies hover and twinkle over the St. Augustine grass. I close my eyes as warmth flows back and forth between our hands. Neither of us has to fill the silence with words. Peace is a new feeling for me. Jack has a spiritual spark inside of him. That has to be positive, as long as he doesn't try to cram me into a religious box. Could that be a new kind of glue that might hold our relationship together?

Jack's phone rings. He ignores it, but with all the turmoil happening around us, I encourage him to see who is calling.

"Hello, Chief. Is everything okay?" He stands up, and my heart drops.

"Nell? When did she … what? Okay, Hope and I will be right there."

I jump up in fear.

"Nell is okay. She got T-boned by someone in a truck who fled the scene."

"*What?*" I shout. "I thought she was in San Antonio!"

"The chief said she cussed a blue streak in the ambulance—scared the EMS guy."

"But she's okay?" I can't stop panting.

"Yes, it could have been much worse. The doctor says rehab will be brutal—put a cramp in Nell's style for a while."

"Don't count on it. Let's go!"

CHAPTER 17

The hushed atmosphere of the hospital waiting room reminds me of my mother's cancer. This Catholic hospital has crucifixes everywhere, just like hers did. Jack and Chief Lindheimer left together on some mission they didn't have time to share and asked if I could stay for a while. Nell is still in recovery, so I have some time to myself.

When I pull out my Mom memories, I find the folder is flimsy—almost empty. Not one to linger or inconvenience anyone, Elizabeth Franklin suffered quietly with her ovaries full of cancer, refusing treatment and dying exactly three months after diagnosis. Even though we were grown, at the funeral Ronny and I stood at her graveside like abandoned children, holding hands, paralyzed with dread as our father tossed a shovelful of dirt over the beautiful white lilies on her coffin.

I want to be angrier about the passive role my mother played in my life, but I don't have the heart to blame her anymore. She gave up her dreams and much of her personality when she married my father—and then finally escaped her personal pain and disappointment through death. I can see that now. Did she pass those genes to me?

When was your last Pap smear?

Very funny, and none of your business. I need you, Oz-God.

Are you crying?

I feel pulled all over the place. Heidi's bombshell, Nell's accident, and Ronny's coming—suddenly, everyone is making decisions without me.

I'm right here.

How will I ever find my way?

If you keep running full tilt, there isn't time to get centered.

When I got like this two months ago, you disappeared, and, I relapsed.

You don't have to look outside yourself to connect to me.

What do you mean?

The potential for all of your answers is already hardwired into your DNA.

If you've always been inside me, part of my DNA …

Awaiting activation and intent.

I don't want to think this hard anymore. I can't figure out what you mean.

Hope Delaney, you are unique. The people in your life, your past experiences, and your sets of strengths and weaknesses are yours—never to be duplicated. The way you and I approach your issues is unique as well.

Then why am I so miserable?

Is this misery or something else?

What do you want me to say—that I love feeling out of control and enjoy the fact that nothing in my life makes sense? It's horrible!

Am I horrible?

I don't know *what* you are.

I love you exactly the way you are.

Then how can you be a part of God?

Consider this: Every piece of writing about Jesus, Muhammad, Gautama Buddha, Confucius, or any master, guru, or prophet was written by a man or woman—a human being—activated by Source.

Not exactly new information.

Every particle of creation is God-breathed.

What you're saying seems to have a frequency that resonates in my soul. Can I trust it?

Don't forget, conscious of it or not, you are a scavenger, prowling down unmarked alleyways or hanging with people who are shunned and judged 'unfit' by many, looking for hidden treasure, for bits and pieces of me. This is part of your soul blueprint, your gift.

"Is every person on a journey toward this?"

Part of the human design is intertwined with the Source, but not all seek this understanding.

I feel very grateful right now. Even though I don't know shit from Shinola, I don't feel alone. Maybe I am letting all this come up because I can finally admit that I need help with it.

Start scavenging where you are. The creed or dogma of any belief can teach important lessons. The spiritual process never ends. Some paths are quicker and more direct than others. Look for love and compassion—they will always lead you forward.

But that means I can't lump anyone, even certain political groups into my box of prejudicial intolerance. Yuck. 'Kumbaya' is not in my skill set.

Arrogance, religious or otherwise, is not part of love.

But I *enjoy* feeling superior.

Ego is predictable that way.

Why do church people think following Jesus is the *only* way?

Jesus, one of the divine/human hybrids?

Have there been other hybrids like him?

Look in the mirror.

Wait, back up a minute! I'm an alien?

Jesus set something into motion, again.

Again?

Christ consciousness is more than Jesus the man, or the religion surrounding him.

What does that mean?

Jesus was a human being born with spiritually activated DNA, 'fathered' by the divine. He didn't come and do what he did to found a religion for only a few, but to show all of humanity what divine activation looks like.

Okay, I'm not sure I understand. Are you saying the only difference between Jesus and me is how activated I am?

Jesus kept telling his disciples that they could communicate with the Source and do the miracles he could do.

So he was saying, 'Here's a shortcut—walk this way?'

Pretty direct message until the inevitable interference of ego and control.

It can't be that simple.

Understanding Christhood was and is like having the touchstone of a new paradigm gently draped across all of creation—the idea that any sin or offense that stands between you and the Source can be balanced and forgiven. Source love is bigger than any horror you could think of committing.

In my little-girl head, whenever I saw images of Jesus nailed to a cross, I never once thought about love. That picture did *not* cause comfort, but fear.

When in reality the act was about ascension out of fear.

So, here in the three-dimensional world, I still have to *process* my story, unravel the knots …

Exactly, if you choose to.

Nothing heavy about that.

I'm a way shower. So are you. All are aspects of the same Source.

Even if I'd been born a Buddhist?

Buddhism wasn't your lesson, not this time.

Wait … what?

A young nurse in Mickey Mouse scrubs interrupts the conversation in my head. "Excuse me. Are you Hope Delaney?"

"Yes, is Nell awake?"

"She sent me to find you. This way …"

CHAPTER 18

Nell has a private room. Her entire left leg is encased in plaster and hanging from a contraption like ones I've seen on television. As I move the visitor's chair next to the bed, the same nurse brings Nell ice water and a cup of lemon Jell-O. After the nurse raises the bed and adjusts the pillows, she leaves with a shy smile, closing the door.

"Your hands are so warm, Hope. I just can't seem to get warm."

In the diffused light, Nell looks pale, her cheeks hollow. I retrieve the extra blanket that is folded at the end of the bed and maneuver it around the cast, tucking it up around her neck and shoulders.

"There ... are you in a lot of pain?" I ask, holding her hands again, under the covers.

"My leg hurts like hell, but with this delightful medication pump, I can maintain a fluffy distance from it," she says, her voice heavy. "I guess God finally got me to slow down." She sighs. "I have such a hard time being still."

"God did this to you?" I ask.

"God didn't *do* this to me—accidents are part of life. He allows us to participate in our lessons."

"Free will can suck," I say.

Nell picks at the loose fibers of the cotton blanket. "I've been running around, wearing myself out, neglecting my husband by trying desperately to help others … exhausting. It looks good because I am working for the Lord, but the truth is, this broken leg is a relief. I just feel sorry for that boy …" Nell draws her brows together.

"What boy?"

"Oh, never mind. Now I remember what I wanted to tell you." Each of Nell's words seems like an effort.

"Why don't you rest now and tell me later?"

"No, this is important! I don't remember why, but it is." She grips my hand. "I told you that I went through a wild time, right?"

"Yes, though I have a hard time believing it."

"Remember, Hope, my worst thing is *my* worst thing. Anyway, one night my daddy sat me down. He was a tough man, but I think he could see I was throwing my life away." Nell pushes the morphine button before continuing. "He said that God gives every baby girl a bottle of heavenly wine when she is born."

I chuckle. "Now that's a belief I can get behind."

Nell smiles and closes her eyes. "Anyway, he said that this wine is supposed to be a wedding gift to our spouses. I guess the wine could also be given to the baby boys, although men always seem to get a pass when it comes to their sexual behavior …" Nell drifts for a moment, and I contemplate slipping out the door, but she jerks awake.

"Are you sure you don't want to take a nap?" I ask.

"No, for some reason I must tell you now. My father said that I could open this bottle of heaven wine before I found my husband and let other men take swigs out of it—could even pass it around indiscriminately—but if I did that, when I found my true mate, all I'd have left would be the dregs, the backwash of other men."

"That's a *horrible* thing to tell you!"

"I thought so too, but he wasn't finished. He took the half-full bottle of wine that I'd been drinking and poured it out in the sink, rinsed it, then filled it with clean water. "'Nellie,' he said, 'do you know what the Good Lord's first miracle was? He turned water into new wine ...'"

CHAPTER 19

The rock band Queen wakes me singing "Another One Bites the Dust," my ringtone for Jack. Through the cracked face of my phone, I see that it is 11:30 a.m.

"Mmm … yes?"

"I waited as long as I could. I know you were up most of the night with Nell."

"What's the matter?" I say, taking the phone back under the covers with me.

"I'm with Heidi and …" Jack pauses, and it sounds like he presses the cell phone against his shirt while he muffle-talks to someone.

A familiar sense of uneasiness drops like the proverbial other shoe.

"Listen, Hope, I'm sorry I woke you, but I have to go. Everything is a fucked right now, but I will fill you in as soon as I can. Don't worry."

"Right. I'll try not to."

"Oh, and Ronny came in last night. I gave him directions to the Pettibone Hotel and your cell number. I love you." Jack hangs up.

"Thus begins the end of Jack," I say to myself.

I wonder if my withholding Heidi's secret, even at her

insistence, will be the lie that destroys our relationship. If she doesn't tell him today, I will. He'll be mad either way— that's guaranteed. My feelings for him are too good to be true anyway.

What are you doing, Hope?
    Preparing.
For the alien-hybrid apocalypse?
    It was stupid of me to believe in fairy tale love.
Why?
    Please don't be a pain, not this morning.
No man can fill the hole in your soul. That's what you told me the other day. A very enlightened moment, I might add.
    If soul mates don't exist, then why do I feel such a deep longing for one?
Everybody wants to feel whole.
    I suppose I'll have to settle for you.
Romantic, right?
    While all my other relationships disintegrate …
Not the plan, Stan.
    Why bother with soul mates at all? We human meatheads could just have indiscriminate sex and babies out here in the physical world and then turn inward and be all goo-goo with you.
Snarky-butt.
    Sorry.
You're afraid, I get that.
    At least one of us does.
What if you and Jack were both tuned in to a higher frequency like here, where you and I connect?
    Then we wouldn't really need each other at all.
Doesn't it make sense that if two people don't have to depend on each other to feel complete, then the relationship becomes one whole person in love with another whole person.

I need to be needed.

That is a neural pathway worth exploring.

What if we're both too far gone to change or Jack doesn't want me anymore?

CHAPTER 20

A white late-model Dodge truck with a smashed grill and one forest-green door is parked in back of the Pettibone Hotel. Must be Ronny's. I hide behind a hedge of Ligustrum, peeking like a stalker. What's wrong with me?

From this vantage point, I can see a dilapidated shed near the truck, almost completely concealed by trees and climbing vines that I haven't noticed before. The building is small but could be cleaned up and used to store extra supplies or yard equipment. Suddenly, a tall skinny teenager in a hoodie darts out of the shed and takes off running – definitely not Ronny, but still familiar somehow.

What the— I emerge from the bushes and look in the direction he ran but see no one.

"Boo!" calls a voice behind me. "Hi, sis."

Ronny has walked up and said just two words, and my heart shatters. I turn to him, and locking our arms around each other, we stand silently, hugging and crying. I *know* this person. Together we share a lifetime of day-to-day survival. Maybe that's why I've been afraid to see him—he might remind me I can't make it on my own.

Finally disentangling, Ronny reaches for a pack of cigarettes in his pocket. In cargo shorts and a dirty David Bowie

T-shirt, he doesn't look crazy or miserable but normal, whatever that means.

"Mind if I smoke?" He fumbles awkwardly with the pack.

"Like one more ash is going to matter around here." I nod my head toward the black-rimmed windows of the second floor. "Don't toss your butts, though. We don't need another bonfire."

"Care to join me?" He offers me one of the filterless camels.

"Of course."

He laughs, and our identically colored eyes meet.

"It's great to see you, sis."

"I know what you mean." Tears threaten to blind me again.

"Nice little project you've got here." Ronny tips his head to the side, and untidy brown hair falls in his eyes, making him look very young and like our mother.

"Are you going to be around long enough to help me with it?" My voice sounds squeaky.

"Maybe, but really, if you want me to leave, I will. By the way, I think Jack is cool. He has a good vibe and a great truck."

"He has a great everything—hands off." I mean the quip as a joke but see his discomfort immediately.

Ronny blows smoke toward the ground. "I told him that surprising you wasn't a good idea, but I really needed to see you, if only for a few hours."

With my arm around his waist, we walk up the front steps of the hotel.

"First off," I say, "I want to apologize for—"

"Accepted. Next?"

"Wait, I need to say this. I've been terrified to see you again, not because I don't care anymore but because I feel guilty and responsible for what happened."

"If you hadn't encouraged me to get honest with myself, I would have self-destructed in some other way."

"But if you had been safe at home, those guys wouldn't have ..."

"Are you saying that our home was *safe*? I was never safe there—neither were you."

"I'm trying to be comforting and take the blame."

"Well, you're bad at it, so stop."

We both laugh, and Ronny drags two wooden crates close together so we can sit.

"I quit drinking," I blurt.

"You're probably real thirsty then."

"Still funny as a crutch," I say.

"Does that mean you've found a higher power?" Ronny's voice sounds bitter and sarcastic.

"Not the kind I expected."

"Are you sure you're 'allowed' to hang out with homosexuals like me?"

"Your mistakes are no different from mine... in the overall scope of things."

"Ahh, so you see being gay as a sin? Mom's friends acted as if I were only a few steps away from pedophiles and serial killers."

"I'm sure those same old biddies judge us fornicators, adulterers, and alcoholics in a similar way."

"You *fornicated*? Off with your head!" Ronny laughs. "With Jack?"

"Shut up!" I elbow Ronny, and he almost falls off of his crate.

"Face it, Hopester—some mistakes are just more acceptable than others. Look at Mom and Dad. She went to church every Sunday, hiding the fact that her husband beat her and sexually abused his children. No one batted an eye at the bruises on her arms."

"I think it's a political issue," I say, picking my fingernail.

"What do you mean?"

"Managing sin is like manipulating the law in your fa-vor—you know, waving a righteous flag and pointing at the offenses you *don't* wrestle with to detract from the ones you *do*."

"If you are suggesting that sins are the same no matter what, you better start running. I see bonfires and pitchforks in your future. Don't you know that gays are doomed if they won't stop being gay?"

"Did you choose it?" I ask.

"Do you mean because of Dad or something? I have a question for you."

"Okay."

"When did you choose to be straight?" Ronny lights an-other cigarette.

"Oh, wow … I never really decided. I just *was*."

"Believe me, Hope, I've thought about the 'why' for years—blamed Dad, became defensive with everyone, cursed God, and then felt cursed *by* God. It would be easy to claim that I am simply just biologically different, but I suspect that my issues are more complex. I think there are as many reasons for being gay as there are gay people."

"When did you get so smart?"

"Years of therapy and a couple of psych classes I'm taking for my LCDC."

"Licensed chemical dependency counselor? I'm so impressed."

"I really have a heart to work with teens in crisis."

"Back to what we were talking about before, I don't think that the source of all love is doing the condemning."

"Well, don't you sound New Age?"

"God isn't about religion, but about relationship."

"Sounds like a tattoo."

"Oh, lookie. I got one, see?"

"Aw, shucks, an itty-bitty heart." Ronny pulls up his T-shirt sleeve and shows me a tattoo of some large Asian-looking characters.

"That's amazing. What does it mean?"

"Fuck off, in Mandarin."

I push him off his crate, and he rolls around in the trash and soot, laughing.

"No, really, Hope, that's what it actually means—or as close as you can get!"

"Actually, it's perfect. I love it. I might have to get an 'itty-bitty' copy of that right on my ass."

"I have so much to tell you, Hope, but before we go any further, there is something I have to know." Ronny's face is stern as he picks up a gallon bottle of Clorox.

"What?"

"Why in the name of all that's holy would you clean antique wooden floors with this?"

CHAPTER 21

"Check this out!" Ronny blows dust off a CD case he found on the kitchen floor. "I'll be damned. It's Johnny Cash's all-time gospel favorites!" When Ronny opens the case, small pieces of paper float to the floor.

"What are those?" I reach toward them.

"You're never going to believe it," Ronny says, holding up one of the pieces to get a closer look. "These are pictures of naked people cut from a magazine."

"Pornography?" I snatch the case from his hands, and more nasty confetti flutters to the floor. "We shouldn't be looking at this."

"Whoa, little sister, what are you, twelve?"

Confused by my prudish shame, I gather the pictures, my face flaming.

Ronny hands me the case, watching me panic. "Dad really did a number on you, didn't he, Hope?"

"Yes, he did. Now come with me to the kitchen and help me with this barrel of broken glass."

"That's got to be some sort of symbol, Hope."

Ronny heaves, and I push, and between us we rock the barrel down the back steps.

"I wonder if there's a wheelbarrow in that shed," Ronny says.

"Speaking of that, did you see anyone hanging around back here before I showed up?"

Ronny shakes his head. "No, why?"

"I saw this kid running away. Let's go check out that shack."

"Aren't you afraid to go in that dark, scary place by yourself?" Ronny raises one eyebrow.

"Don't start. I'm no longer a child."

"Maybe an old crone with claw hands and witch moles is hiding in there," Ronny cackles.

I run away from him and tear open the shed door as if daring my childhood fears to manifest. "Oh my God, Ronny, look at this."

A partially burned overstuffed chair is covered with a filthy Ninja Turtles blanket. A wooden cable spool is turned on its side like an end table and covered with an assortment of empty beer bottles.

Ronny picks one up and reads the label. "Our hideaway likes fancy IPA beer. Maybe the cut out nudie pics came from this stack of magazines."

"They seem to be mostly of men," I say.

"Look at these bullets all over the floor. Here's the box, they're for a .38—the kind Dad used in his police revolver. I think we've stumbled onto someone's secret." Ronny looks around with sadness on his face, as if he recognizes the place or remembers one similar to it.

"Do you see a gun that goes with these bullets?" My chest feels tight.

"I need some air." Ronny slams out the door.

I follow my brother outside and find him leaning against the old Dodge, pale and wobbly.

"Do you want some water or something?" I ask.

"You said it was a boy who ran out of here this morning?"

"Yes, a tall, gangly boy in a hoodie ... Wait, I think I might know who it is. Are you okay to drive me somewhere?"

"Hope, don't you have a car?"

"Yes, but I walked over here this morning after breakfast."

"I would drive, but I don't have my wheels, either. Jack dropped me off this morning and said you could take me back to my hotel."

"This isn't your truck?"

"No, it was already parked when I got here."

CHAPTER 22

My call to Jack goes straight to voice mail.

"Ronny, I know where we might find help, but we'll have to walk a few blocks—unless you want to hot-wire this piece-of-shit truck."

"Don't have to. The keys are in it. Gotta love small towns."

"Well, I'm not stealing a car. I just got my driver's license back."

"You had a DUI?"

"Yes, yes. I got really drunk a couple of months ago and spent the night in jail. That's why I was 'let go' from my university job. Impressed?"

"What's impressive is just how badly you've screwed up since I last saw you!"

"Just shut up and drive, asshole. If we get in trouble, I'm going to say that you forced me into the car."

"Where to, ma'am?"

"Take a left up here and go a few blocks … over there, the Cactus Café."

"That's where Jack and I ate breakfast—the best blueberry pancakes ever."

We park across the street. It's only 4:30 p.m., but the "Closed" sign has been turned around. I see movement inside even though the interior lights are off. Nothing about this feels right.

"Do you know if there's a back entrance?" Ronny asks.

"I'm sure there is, but I've never seen it. Come on, don't look in the windows when we pass."

The alley is abandoned and smells like bacon grease and garbage. The black metal door to the café is unlocked.

I grab Ronny's arm before we go in. "Remember that Russell—that's the teenager I saw running away—may be drunk and have a gun."

"Yes, but he's also just a mixed-up kid," Ronny adds.

I can't believe we are walking into such a loaded situation. Usually, the crises are about me, my own tornadoes and snakebites. I send an SOS to Oz-God—just in case he wants to rally some angel warriors or something.

"Ms. Patty? Hello? Is anyone here?" We walk past the grill into the restaurant, and four serious faces turn toward us.

Jack stands up and comes to me with concern. "What are you doing here, Hope?"

"I don't know who you guys are, but Uncle Jack, you better tell them to sit the fuck down." Russell has backed himself into a corner facing the front door and has his right hand in his hoodie pocket, with what looks like the muzzle of a pistol pressed against the fabric.

"Oh my God, Jack. Does that boy have a gun pointed at us?"

Jack nods and guides me over to sit at the counter. Ronny stands beside us.

Heidi and her mom are seated across from each other at one of the booths. Heidi's eyes are swollen and glazed.

"I guess I can't call you *Uncle* Jack anymore." Russell shakes his head, anger turning his neck and cheeks bright red. "This sucks so bad. You're all such lying losers."

Jack clenches his jaw and stares at the counter. I recognize the look of shame and defeat on his face.

"Just so you know, Russell, I'm Hope, and this is my brother Ronny."

Ronny walks toward the boy with his hand outstretched.

"Stop right there, faggot. I heard my dad talking about you last night."

"Ronny!" Heidi gives her son a stern look, but he refuses to meet her gaze.

"Hey, all faggots go to hell, right, Grandma?" Russell pulls the gun out of his pocket and tries to control his shaking hand by resting it on the table.

"Okay, Russell, we're listening to you. Just take it easy," Jack says, raising both hands.

"Is that how you screwed my mom? Was she easy?"

With every word her grandson says, Patty's face becomes stonier, her knuckles white from clenching her fists.

"Well, maybe," I say breathlessly, my hands waving, "we're all going to hell!"

All eyes move from Russell's gun to me. "Let's see. In this room we have a gay man, at least two alcoholics, quite a few fornicators and adulterers, a truck thief ..." I raise my eyebrows at Russell, and he looks sideways. "We have abortion, lust, greed—am I missing anything?"

"Now wait just a minute." Patty stands up and crosses her arms. "I've never done any of those things."

Heidi turns slowly to stare at her mother. The anger emanating from her is almost as thick and hot as her son's, and I find myself holding my breath.

"Well, *Mother*, I do remember the Bible saying something about self-righteous, arrogant church ladies who think they are better than everyone else."

Patty, shocked into silence, stumbles back into her seat and stares out the window. I nod at Heidi, resisting the desire to high-five her in front of everyone.

"You forgot to add 'liars' to the list." Russell brings us all back to the moment.

"Pretty important, don't you think, Mom? My whole fucking life has been a lie!"

"Honor thy mother and father," Patty mumbles, blowing her nose into a wad of paper napkins.

"Why should I honor my parents, Gram, after all the shit …" Russell's voice cracks.

"Not you, Russy. Me," Patty says with defiance. "That's the commandment I broke. I hated my mother and skipped church a few times. There, are y'all happy?"

"Welcome to the party, Mom." Heidi reaches across the table and holds her mother's hand.

Jack, still seated on the stool next to mine, has barely taken his eyes off his son. "Where did you get the gun, Russell?" he asks in a cool voice.

"Grandpa's workshop is full of surprises."

"I bet your grandpa's shop has a refrigerator full of IPA beer, How can you stand that hopped-up taste?" says Ronny, who casually maneuvers his way closer to Russell.

"Yeah, beggars can't be choosers." Russell sits up, takes the gun in both hands, and points it at the floor, like his father and grandfather probably taught him. "Frankly, I don't give a shit anymore. I'm done with all of you."

Jack's leg is touching mine, and I feel his thigh muscles tense, getting ready to spring. I pray for angelic intervention.

"Mom, tell Dad … I mean *Charlie* …"

Before Russell can finish, the front door crashes open, and Deputy Portnoy yells, "Drop your weapon!"

Out of sheer reflex, Russell raises the gun, and Ronny dives for it.

CHAPTER 23

My ears are ringing, muffling the sounds of screams, as Jack tackles Russell and pins him to the ground. I crawl to Ronny—so much blood spreading across his T-shirt.

"Ronny? Can you hear me? Ronny! Open your eyes, damn it!"

Patty kneels beside me with a roll of paper towels while looking for the source of the bleeding, as if battlefield medicine is what she's born for.

Jack and the deputy walk Russell out the door in handcuffs as Heidi, white-faced, trails behind them.

I barely remember getting to the hospital. For some reason there isn't enough room in the ambulance for me to go with Ronny. Patty drives me in the beat-up truck, managing to dig three Advil out of her purse and hand them to me while shifting gears. Even though I have no injuries, I swallow them with no water.

I give the ER nurses as much information about my brother as I can and then watch helplessly as they roll him through the swinging doors into surgery. Déjà vu envelops me, and Patty steers me down the hall away from the ER and into the hospital chapel.

"Hope, you sit a while. It's safe in here, and nobody's going to ask you any more stupid questions." Patty seems to not know what to do with her hands. "I need to call my husband now ..."

"Oh, of course ... Thank you so much for the Advil. I'll be fine." I slide into the pew and muster a smile as Patty disappears on silent orthopedic shoes.

CHAPTER 24

The chapel is small but maintains the rudiments of a church—a tiny altar area and three short rows of pews divided by an aisle. When I came to see Nell before, I didn't notice it. A good-sized crucifix hangs front and center, and a tall red candle burns on a small table off to the side. I have an impulse to blow the candle out.

I stare at the face of the man hanging on the cross, being tortured to death. The low light and flickering candle play tricks, animating the pain on his face. Blood-red anger rises inside me.

No, Oz-God, just no! I am *so* done with all of this. Ronny *again*? What the hell are you doing to him, to all of us? This spiritual BS has no meaning—I don't get it, and I don't get you!

There isn't much light for you in here. Do you want to walk outside?

You act as if you're different from them, but you have been manipulating me all along so you can just nail me up there with your other aliens!

Them who?

I don't know. You and the other ones who believe and pretend to care. I wave my hand toward the altar. Since I first heard you at the beach, you've seduced me with supernatural affection and understanding, trying to trick me into accepting this. I knew it couldn't be real. Oh no. I really am mentally ill.

So because of what happened at the café, you've lumped me in with all the humans who have let you down and abandoned and abused you for their own selfish reasons?

Well, if the wings fit. Once again, you didn't protect us, and now Ronny is critically injured, Jack's world has been ripped open, and I'm … well, I'm furious and just know you're behind it all!

How will blaming me change this experience?

Everyone I love gets tangled up in turmoil. How can that be an accident?

I love the smell of turmoil in the morning …

See? You don't even *care*. Our misery makes you happy! Just when my life starts to balance, *bam!* The rolling handcart to hell arrives at my door. Hop in, time for another freaking sacrifice!

Out of chaos comes order … it's kinda my thing.

You're sicker than I thought. I'm not sure I want anything to do with you.

I know you can't see it right now but, we are bringing light to the pandemonium.

Why is life so screwed? From birth to death there is screaming—loved ones hurt you, plans go awry, everything seems dirty, heavy, and painful, and you act all happy-go-lucky as if this is *normal*.

Growth is normal, and I will walk with you through everything that happens, even if you never speak to me again.

So I *can* blame you for this shit show!

Oh yes, and then your ego sets a huge juicy steak of self-righteous offense on your plate like a reward—proof that you've done nothing wrong and couldn't possibly be responsible for any of the pain in your life.

You are supposed to be loving and compassionate to me.

I'm sick of your lectures. None of what happened in the café *was* my fault, for once. Is Ronny going to die just because he came to visit me?

He isn't dying. The bullet passed through the muscle of his upper arm.

But, why? It could have killed him!

If you had five Post-it notes lined up in front of you labeled with the names Heidi, Charlie, Russell, Jack, and Ronny, could you see any other chaos that led to Russell's gun going off?

Maybe I should have stayed with Ronny at the Pettibone and let them handle their own consequences.

Why did *you go to the café searching for Jack?*

Because I care so much … and was worried about him. Even though we haven't been together long, I knew that finding out about Russell would pierce Jack to the bone.

Love and compassion.

I can see a few obvious things, that is, if I were to jot down notes on each person's piece of paper.

Okay …

I don't get to escape the self work by analyzing them, do I?

What would be the fun in that? Their behavior will mirror some of your own.

Sicko. Well, in Jack's case, Russell is a simple consequence of a reckless choice he made one spring break. I know there's more to it, but I'm trying to condense this into something I can manage.

What about Ronny?

Maybe his immediate identification with Russell's anger and disillusion caused Ronny's wounds to break open, releasing an instinctive need to rush in and save the boy.

What else?

Heidi's lie about her son's birth father has caused a ripple of deceit to rock her world, crashing over Charlie, Jack, and Russell in a wave of pain she never imagined.

Why do you think she lied?

Fear. Like Annabelle Pettibone, she must have been mortified, afraid of being cast out and condemned by the church, her family, and all those she loved.

Out of the darkness comes light. Sometimes you are the victim, sometimes you do the damage, and sometimes you bring the intention of love to the situation.

"Oh yeah, I really saved the day.

Can you hear that ticking sound?

Must be the bomb in my chest about to blow all my bullshit to smithereens!

I'm listening to the millions of tiny synapses going off in your brain—causing extreme emotions, making connections, overlapping, reconfiguring, zipping up the dead ideas and birthing the new, all happening while you try to swallow your own bitter medicine.

My brain is always farting and obsessing. What's different now?

You tell me.

Do you remember yesterday evening when Jack and I were enjoying the sunset?

Such fun … making cloud art is quite popular in this dimension.

Yes! The sun was shining through holes in the clouds with penetrating beams. My mother used to tell us that's when angels with flashlights were searching for souls to save.

That is a sweet memory. Why are you so sad?

You mean aside from the fact that, once again, I'm keeping a hospital vigil for Ronny?

Yes, aside from that.

I feel as if my heart has been trapped inside a black box for eons, separated and alone, surrounded by cave-like darkness … Then you punched a hole in the box top and found me crouching there.

Peekaboo.

You've given me my own little spotlight to stand in, but I'm still afraid. Just beyond my circle of illumination, incomprehensible evil lurks, snatching at me like a peace-eating vampire, just waiting for another eclipse. Please don't leave me!

I'm part of you.

Help me understand.

Your metaphor is incomplete.

What do you mean?

Close your eyes. Imagine that you are inside your box of darkness under the beam of Source love. Allow your higher self or imagination to show you what it wants. Just pretend—there is no right answer.

All right … I trust you.

What do you see?

I'm not alone in there. I can see people from my childhood church huddled together under a different light beam. They look afraid too. There are other beams … other people, alone or in groups.

What do you think it means?

The darkness is thick and cold. I see my mistakes and painful memories outside of the light, as you described before … being recorded, almost fondled, by beings not fueled by love.

You have been brave, reaching into that darkness and wrestling a few of those memories and events out of darkness and into view where we can look at them.

But what happens to the memories after that?

Once we process something together, it travels up the light beam to me and is transmuted. Even if you have to experience different aspects of the same event or forgive someone hundreds of times, once something has our cosmic coding attached to it, evil no longer has access to it, ever.

I also see that some of the groups are beckoning for me to join them, saying that my light isn't pure—that I may have been deceived and need to be with them, under their light. Is that true? Are you tricking me, Oz-God? Is what we have false and a product of evil?

What does your heart say?

That there are as many ways of being with you as there are humans on the earth.

Most children go to school for twelve years, right?

In America we are lucky.

'The journey of a thousand miles begins with a single step.'

I've heard that one. Are you quoting Laozi?

One step taken on the spiritual highway is a step further along the spiritual highway.

Deep … yet foolishly simple.

When the judgment of others is removed, the loving light in the universe can shine through. Whatever grade or level of learning someone else is experiencing remains none of your business. You have your own lessons to learn.

What about helping others? That is a rock solid standard of everything I've studied.

Define help. It's not your job to change a person's mind or try and fix their problems for them. Love and listen.

This is interesting …

What?

These groups under light beams in this mental exercise seem to be a variety of organized religions and different types of believers.

My love pierces the darkness. Focus on that.

Now I'm even more confused. Which ways are right and have your endorsement?

What do you think is outside of the box—which, by the way, contains not only a select few but all of humanity?

I'd like to think that light and love—basically, God—is outside shining in through all the holes and cracks.

Look to the group standing under the beam to your left. What do you think would happen if you reached your hand across the darkness?

To pull them over to my way?

No, just imagine holding someone's hand across the darkness.

Oh, wow, now our lights are merging, but I don't know who they are or what they believe. What happens to my ideas, and to my unique relationship with you? Won't we both be absorbed or have to convert to some other way of believing? What if *they* are the ones who have been deceived? Will they infect me?

And here you see how black-and-white thinking has infiltrated religion and caused separation through judgment rather than unity through love.

At some higher dimensional level, is there truth within both polarities? I mean, one person's white is another's black.

Both polarities exist in every religion, political party, and so on, but choosing one extreme or definition of reality without exploring or understanding the opposite expression causes disharmony, imbalance, and chaos.

Chaos, your favorite.

Only because it can lead to a higher order. The same dynamic has been happening inside you. If pain and fear is suppressed, ignored or 'blamed away,' there is no way to escape slavery.

Is that the goal—escaping the box? What's outside, heaven, nirvana, enlightenment?

From inside the box it is hard to imagine being free from the concept of punishment and reward—to be free of judgment and discrimination without dying or converting everyone to your way of believing.

My mother kept preaching to us that obedience and good works lead souls to heaven. I think that is why she stayed with my father.

The so-called kingdom isn't somewhere out there separate from you, but a structural part of the blueprint of your DNA—available inside.

You sound very heretical, right now. One for all and all for one? I may not be a religious type but all of this acceptance and handholding across the aisle goes against millennia of programming.

You do need to ask for the relationship with me, however. That's one of the 'heretical' concepts that Jesus, brought to the table.

I don't want to be trapped in the box anymore, but why do I feel as if I'm only one small step from another, more insidious Kool-Aid machine?

You and I are speaking a new language, a spirit language that carries new codes from the heart of God.

If I'm connected to your light through the hole you poked into my dark world, can't I just travel up the beam and be free of the box altogether?

Every time we talk, you leave the box.

Really? But then afterwards, I wave goodbye to you and jump back down the rabbit hole. Why do I keep doing that?

Don't be so hard on yourself, Hope. Evolution is a process. Start where you are. While you are in the box, examine your relationships, pay attention to every event that happens, and let the memories and feelings arise into the light. Don't be afraid to walk up to other huddled seekers and ask them what they know— exchange treasures.

What do I do with their judgment … and mine? I'm afraid they won't interact with me unless I pretend to believe their way. I won't do that.

Love exists outside of humanity's definition of it. Every time you reach out intending to increase the light in your personal world, you become quantumly entangled with others. Each of those other beings holds a spark of the Source—look for it.

I guess that means, my dad, my exes, and all the other losers in my life.

Don't get overwhelmed. Just take one loser at a time.

I have a really long way to go … pretty damn humbling.

Eventually, the darkness will disintegrate completely, and all of humanity will ascend out of the box.

So I should continue the way I'm headed?

What's your intent, Hope?

To bug the hell out of you forever.

CHAPTER 25

I've been sitting on an ivy-covered railroad trestle, swinging my legs above the flowing river. I spent hours waiting at the hospital, until Ronny was moved out of ICU and into a private room. I held his hand for a while and then left him sleeping. Profoundly exhausted and emotionally shredded, I felt compelled to sneak away and find somewhere I could breathe fresh air.

I hear the crunch of gravel as a truck drives up and parks outside of my view. Suddenly, Jack crashes through the brush on the riverbank below. How did he know where I went? Maybe he isn't looking for me but has his own demons chasing him.

Even from above, I see that his shoulder muscles are bunched and his leg movements are jerky as he paces back and forth. He picks up a small flat stone, and with a style and force perfected over a lifetime, he sends the rock skipping over the surface of the water. The second rock flies so hard and fast that it sails completely over the river and smacks into a cypress tree on the far side.

When I stand up, the movement catches his eye. He strides toward the trestle and scrambles toward me. He isn't smiling, and I feel a spike of fear at the intensity in his face. His hair is wild, and the exertion of climbing causes his chest to heave, the perspiration making him look slick and dangerous.

"Where did you go, Hope? God, I need you so badly."

Without waiting for me to respond, Jack pulls me roughly against him, kissing me, demanding that I surrender to his hunger, which unleashes my own. All lofty thoughts and good intentions vaporize as our souls and bodies strain to be closer.

"Jack, I can't breathe …"

"I don't care, Hope. I want you. Nothing else matters."

His words make my thoughts thick and slow like lava or molten gold escaping from the earth's core, and his hands radiate a feverish heat through my shirt.

"Slow down, Jack, please … This isn't like you." I put my fists against his chest to keep him at a distance while I catch my breath.

"You're wrong, Hope. This is exactly like me. I'm tired of pretending to be an upstanding and respectful boyfriend. I'm not. It's you who are in danger and should get away from me." His mouth on my neck further erodes my will to resist him.

"Oh God, help me," I whisper.

My helpless plea breaks through Jack's passion, and he pulls back, rigid and stunned, his eyes moving from side to side as if he is being chased by an unseen predator.

"Oh my God, I'm so sorry, Hope. I didn't mean … or maybe I did. I'm so angry and confused right now."

He looks as if he might bolt toward his truck, so I gently wrap my arms around his waist and lean against him, slowly stroking his back and willing his ragged breathing to slow down.

"I'll tell you what, Jack. I'm just glad we didn't meet while we were both drinking." I interlace my fingers with his and lean against the rusted bridge railing.

"It might have been simpler then," he says, looking at the ground. "Slam, bam, and thank you, ma'am."

"I don't think so. Without any restraints, we might have caused an earthquake somewhere. Good Lord, man, you are something else!" I lift my hair and fan the back of my neck.

He flashes me an awkward smile, but the serious sadness returns almost immediately. "I have this craziness inside me, and sex is only one of the ways it blows up sometimes. I spiral into a place of resentment about ... the list is too long to drag out. I guess I feel cheated in life, and when critical mass is reached ..."

"Like finding out about Russell?"

"I go nuts and start acting out, being destructive, demanding my way."

"I'm sure you noticed just now that I had no trouble jumping on your lust wagon."

Jack smiles and gives me a sexy side-eye. "Talk about hot ... Jeez, girl, I can just imagine what—"

"Stop talking immediately!"

Jack laughs at my awkward blushing. "You know, Hope, while my ego is always flattered by the way women respond to me, just look at the damage I've done."

"Join the crowd."

"With my carelessness, I ruined Heidi's life and her marriage and set up Russell, my own son, for misery. They all have reasons to hate me, and I don't know what to do next."

"Heidi wasn't married when you had your fling. Why should they all hate you? Yes, it became a mess, but it was Heidi who lied."

"Russell hates me, I could see it in his eyes."

"Russell hates everyone right now. You guys will eventually work this out. You won't rest until you do."

I nod my head and watch him pace, not able to interrupt his descent into the dark feelings.

"For the first time in my life, I don't have a plan. I'm not sure I've ever felt this panicked. What do I do?"

"About Russell?"

"Not just that. Us too. I was just about to throw you down on these wooden planks, which has nothing to do with the respect I really feel for you. I love you, Hope, more than anyone else I've known."

Jack puts his fingers gently under my chin and stares into my eyes, his own eyes searching for a connection to my essence with as much intensity as his mouth on mine. I feel something almost painful, an ache in my breasts not related to sex. It is something else, a far deeper and unfamiliar feeling.

"I've wanted to tell you the same thing," I admit, "but all the love words seem so lame and empty. My feelings are confusing and terrifying. I'm a very twisted-up person when it comes to love. Just sayin'."

Jack kisses my cheek. "We're quite a pair, eh?"

"Part of me believes that something this powerful can't be all wrong."

"Are you talking about sexual attraction or our relationship?"

"Maybe we're just used to skipping over the love and respect steps and diving right into the fire."

"I did the same thing with alcohol, with work, even with sobriety—skipping the steps until something blows up in my face." Jack struggles with his words. "It always blows up. Maybe we should just get married."

"Whoa now, cowboy. We really don't even know each other …"

"That is such bullshit. I may not know the details of your whole life, but I know you, Hope, deep in my gut."

"Do we have to immediately jump into forever after? I know sexual angst is fun and all, but maybe we can view this relationship like we're having a five-course dinner, with lots of talking. Besides, we both have some urgent family issues we need to untangle right now."

"I guess I could try eating the steak and vegetables before binging on dessert, but ..."

"Why is that the heaviest 'but' I've ever heard?"

"Because I know almost nothing about healthy eating, and I'm addicted to sweets."

CHAPTER 26

"Let's walk down by the river, okay?" Jack helps me down the steep riverbank, and we sit on a log by the water.

"You know that Heidi made me promise not to say anything to you about Russell until she had a chance," I say. "Can you forgive me?"

"I've had my fill of deception." Jack gives me a sideways glance. "But I suppose it was Heidi's secret to tell. I'm just glad Ronny is okay. Funny how we're all knotted up together in this."

"I was thinking the same thing earlier. What is Chief Lindheimer going to do with Russell?" I ask, changing the subject.

"I don't know. I sat with Russell in the jail, but he wouldn't talk to me ... wanted me to leave him alone."

"Was it Russell who hit Nell with that truck?"

"Unfortunately, yes. The truck belongs to a man who helps Jake and Patty with their yard work. Heidi figures Russell ran to his grandparents' house after she told him I was his birth father and drank quite a few of Grandpa's beers and then 'borrowed' the truck and wrecked into Nell."

"Nell knew it was Russell."

"Yes, she finally admitted that she saw his face. I guess

Russ hid out in the shed behind the Pettibone. No one knew where he was for over twenty-four hours."

"I thought the truck was Ronny's. What a nightmare."

The sound of the water is soothing, different from the power of ocean waves yet still a medium for healing.

"Jack, were you surprised … about Russell?" I ask.

"Are you kidding? Came totally out of left field. But then again, today when I saw him with that gun, so angry and hurt, it was like looking at a reflection of myself. He looks so much like me. How could I have been so dim? Heidi should have told me."

"What would you have done?"

"Probably tried to marry her."

"Do you love her, Jack?"

"We grew up together. Of course, I love her."

"Like a wife?" I ask in a small voice.

"I don't believe in abandoning my responsibilities. As I told you before, I've spent most of my adult life trying to undo an impressive string of bad choices."

"I don't think Russell is a bad choice." I take Jack's restless hand. "At least Heidi didn't kill her unborn child."

Jack scans my face until he senses what I mean. "Oh, babe, I'm so sorry. Come here."

"Oh, Jack, I've done so many awful things."

"I have to believe we'll get better." Jack holds me, swaying slightly. "Besides, it's only been a little over a month since that tornado forced us into that crumbling adobe fireplace."

"Still the best first date ever. You've ruined me for anyone else."

"I hope so." Jack kisses me gently on the lips.

"I have to confess something," I say. "I've been having these experiences, you know, kind of God-ish—well, something more spiritual than what I thought God was, more ghostlike. Oh, never mind. Just so you know I'm not a total heathen."

"Ghosts? Have you been flirtin' with the devil?"

"Don't say that!" I blush with frustration.

"I'm just teasing you.

"But I'm not religious."

"It doesn't matter to me."

"I mean it!"

"Okay, Hope, duly noted. Now come with me. I want to show you something." Jack drags me through weeds beside the river. "Look."

In the ancient limestone riverbank are three adult dinosaur tracks in a row. One edge has cracked off into the water, but I can still see a few baby tracks beside the bigger ones.

"Are those real?" I crouch down and put my hand completely inside one of the three-toed footprints.

"Just south of Fort Worth on the Paluxy River, they supposedly found dinosaur tracks like these next to some human footprints. Wouldn't that be something?"

"Yes, even one fossil could rewrite all we know about history. Millions and millions of years are more than my pea brain can contemplate. Those years could have held eons of alien habitation, evolution, and then destruction. One asteroid hits the earth, and everything sinks beneath the ocean or gets covered in lava and volcanic ash, and we have to begin again."

Jack laughs, sending another rock flying across the water. "I knew I could count on you, Hope."

"What do you mean?"

"You're curious—sometimes freaky and fearful, but you took my idea about the dinosaurs and ran with it, much further than I dreamed. I love that about you."

"Well, why did you bring up the subject in the first place?"

"I'm not sure. It's interesting to imagine a million-year-old dinosaur just walking along this same river with its baby … 'Doo-de-doo, let's kick some ass.'"

"Doo-de-doo?" I say with sarcasm. "Sounds like something Oz-God would say."

"Oz-God?"

"Never mind."

"No more secrets, from *any* of you bitches!" Jack says with a bit too much force.

"It sounds as if you still have some unprocessed anger at women."

"Don't change the subject. You aren't getting out of this. Who is Oz-God?" Jack wraps a long arm around me as we walk.

"Part of what I was trying to say before. There are some things you may not want to know about me too—the crazy-sounding things."

"Is Oz-God your imaginary friend?"

"Kind of, although I'm beginning to think that my relationship with ... this friend is not so imaginary."

"Wait, like Wizard of Oz God? The man behind the curtain?" Jack says.

"You got my movie metaphor ... I might weep." I sigh and lean against him.

"I'll bet nobody remembers that movie as well as I do. I must have worn out two or three VHS tapes of it."

"My first nightmare was about the Tin Man."

"Do you still remember it?" he asks.

"I was a toddler, and I knew the Tin Man was in my closet, pounding on his empty, heartless chest. Do you remember that sound? The loneliness of it sent me crying to my mother."

"Does Oz-God have something in his black bag for you?" Jack smiles but is no longer teasing.

"Yeah, he's helping me find my way back home."

Jack takes my face in his calloused hands. "Hope, we have a few golden threads of something real, gathered from here and there. If we wind them together—"

"But if you knew how screwed-up I really am …"

"Don't you see? We share that. Our past wretchedness changes into something else when we're together. Don't you feel it? I know God has me by the scruff of the neck, but the details of what that means are confusing. In some ways, I'm not as spiritual as you, Hope."

"That's so funny." I shake my head.

"Why?"

"Do you really think I have any semblance of my shit together in this area?"

"Ronny told me last night that he really wants to help with the adolescent home."

"He wants to help me, or run it himself? When did this happen? Did he talk to Nell?" I ask.

"You aren't the only one with inside connections. By the way, what does Oz-God say about me?" Jack smiles and puffs out his chest.

"Why don't you ask him yourself?"

CHAPTER 27

No matter how much I try to think of something serious, laughter consumes me. I giggle in the shower and after, while scrambling eggs for my dinner. When I think of Jack, Heidi and Russell, Ronny, or the future—basically *everything* leading to or from this moment—inexplicable joy bubbles up through my habitual fear, and I crack up again.

Jack is right—each strand, person, insight, and mistake is part of our quantum entanglement with life, a stanza of music from the sonata of hope that Oz-God is teaching me to sing. With wisdom comes pain. I knew that already. What has set my heart on fire is the discovery that through this pain comes the joy of digging up buried treasure, a resurrection from my dead past.

Jack and I will learn about love and make some mistakes, Ronny and the rest of us will struggle toward healing, and I will continue to ask hard questions. This makes me smile. Source God, Heavenly Father Being, Oz-God or whatever facet I'm connected to during this stage of my journey, loves me in my unfinished state.

This invisible force that I don't understand has handed Jack and me a fractal of the puzzle that might take us years to figure out. What fun, as long as I don't have to do it alone. My journey isn't wrong or weak or something I need to judge as failure, but part of fulfilling the deepest desires of my heart— evidence of creative design.

However, not being able to control the future or know what I'm supposed to do with my life still makes me nuts.

Tolerating ambiguity is the beginning of ascension.

What do you mean by, ascension? Am I dying soon? And besides, isn't making goals a good thing?

Send your plans and requests out to us, we who love you and want the best for you. Then release your attachment to the how and when. Sometimes, forcing things to happen the way you have envisioned them interferes with receiving something even better.

So even if my intentions are good, they may not be the best plan for me?

Many people dance on this edge until they die..

What edge?

Surrendering control enough to manifest their dreams.

Define control.

Slow down.

Okay, I'm breathing … in … out … in …

Not just your breath. Everything. Give your relationships with Jack and Ronny some time. Talk and listen, and respect each other's processes through these hard issues. Just remember, kindness and patience triumph over judgment.

You're speaking that foreign language again.

Remember when you first heard my voice?

We've come such a long way since then. I was so hung up on trying to disprove the Bible and catch you in some sort of lie. You seemed different too. What's that about?

A lot had to do with your expectation of God, as the judgmental punisher that you had completely rejected. We started where you were with the perceptions you grew up with.

So our relationship evolves, too?

If you let it.

You're not supposed to ever change.
I don't, you do.
Well that explains a lot.
What do you mean?
How your 'voice' changed from Old Testament to New.
Close your eyes and imagine our beach. Describe what you see.
The water is green and clear, fading slightly where it meets the sky in a long endless line, the crack where I slipped into your dimension. I imagine a warm, damp breeze on my cheeks, and I smell salt and sea oats after a rain. The sounds of many waves blend together like a roar of excited voices, each anxious to tell their story.
Look at the sand.
It's pinkish-gray, the way it looks at sunrise and sunset. I see billions of sparkles that catch the light.
What is your next step?
Going to the beach? Looking for the sparkle in others?
Start in your own backyard.
I know what it's like to feel no sparkle.
You don't quite remember who you are yet.
Remember? At some time in the past, did I know who I was?
That's another story.
I don't know how to do what you're asking.
I have an endless supply of glitter.
What are you talking about?
Your words, your touch, and even your footsteps leave a tangible mark on the earth.
You know I'm still gonna cuss and screw up in some colossal ways?
Forgiveness glitters too.
Do you remember when I was in college?
Do you?
Ha-ha. I bought an American flag at a thrift store. The

storeowner said, that it had flown for a day over the Capitol in DC. I safety-pinned it around me like a patriotic sarong—probably very illegal—put on my cowboy boots, and went to a Halloween party.

Oh, say, can you see?

The hostess rolled out a ten-foot piece of blank canvas on the kitchen floor and gave us all types of art stuff—paint, markers, chalk, glitter, glue, et cetera—to 'make our mark.'

You danced quite a bit.

I did! Got sweaty and covered my whole body with glitter and proceeded to hug and smear sparkles on everyone at the party.

Not all were receptive.

Yes, well, quite a few tequila shots were involved. But the coolest part was afterward. For a week or two, some of the partygoers told me that glitter kept showing up in the most unusual places—on their bodies, in the shower, their beds, their cars, and even on clean laundry.

A vision of things to come …

I'm still writing down our story but …

But?

I'm afraid.

Go on.

I'll probably piss off a ton of people. Even if I pretend to be tough and 'over' what other people think of me. I'm insecure mush inside.

Who are your friends?

Other rebellious stinkers.

What if this whole conversation is just for you and me?

And Ronny. He wants to hear all about you, even if it's just to tease me about it.

And then there were two …

I need to release my attachment to the outcome of writing this story down?

Again, what do you want, Hope?

To keep scavenging.

It isn't about what you do, but about who we are becoming together that opens a vortex in the space-time continuum.

That's what I want.

When you become afraid of being honest or let others ridicule and reject your personal experience, remember, this is our *story—our unique adventure.*

So not necessarily for anyone else?

This type of processing takes courage.

Whew! Then no one has to take me seriously?

I love you, stinker.

Thank you, thank you, thank you!

What for?

This moment.

Only this *moment?*

This one too.

You comprehend much, grasshopper.

To infinity?

And beyond!

ABOUT THE AUTHOR

Mary-Keith Dickinson is a counselor, artist, and spiritual "wayshower" with a heart for spreading psycho-spiritual enlightenment. With degrees in art and psychology, she has been a professional organizer and holistic life coach involved in twelve-step work and mind/body healing for over twenty years. She has two grown children and lives in the Texas Hill Country with her husband.

Printed in the United States
By Bookmasters